Securing Jane

Also From Susan Stoker

SEAL of Protection: Legacy Series:
Securing Caite
Securing Brenae
Securing Sidney
Securing Piper
Securing Zoey
Securing Avery
Securing Kalee
Securing Jane

SEAL Team Hawaii Series
Finding Elodie (Apr 2021)
Finding Lexie (Aug 2021)
Finding Kenna (Oct 2021)
Finding Monica (TBA)
Finding Carly (TBA)
Finding Ashlyn (TBA)
Finding Jodelle (TBA)

SEAL of Protection Series:
Protecting Caroline
Protecting Alabama
Protecting Alabama's Kids
Protecting Fiona
Marrying Caroline (novella)
Protecting Summer
Protecting Cheyenne
Protecting Jessyka
Protecting Julie (novella)
Protecting Melody
Protecting the Future
Protecting Alabama's Kids (novella)
Protecting Kiera (novella)
Protecting Dakota

Shielding Sierra (TBA)

Ace Security Series:
Claiming Grace
Claiming Alexis
Claiming Bailey
Claiming Felicity
Claiming Sarah

Mountain Mercenaries Series:
Defending Allye
Defending Chloe
Defending Morgan
Defending Harlow
Defending Everly
Defending Zara
Defending Raven

Silverstone Series
Trusting Skylar (Dec 2020)
Trusting Taylor (Mar 2021)
Trusting Molly (July 2021)
Trusting Cassidy (Dec 2021)

Stand-Alone:
The Guardian Mist
Nature's Rift
A Princess for Cale
A Moment in Time
Lambert's Lady

Beyond Reality Series:
Outback Hearts
Flaming Hearts
Frozen Hearts

Securing Jane

A SEAL of Protection:
Legacy Series Novella

By Susan Stoker

1001 DARK NIGHTS
PRESS

Securing Jane
A SEAL of Protection: Legacy Series Novella

Copyright 2021 Susan Stoker

ISBN: 978-1-951812-33-1

Published by 1001 Dark Nights Press, an imprint of Evil Eye Concepts, Incorporated

One Thousand and One Dark Nights

Once upon a time, in the future…

*I was a student fascinated with stories and learning.
I studied philosophy, poetry, history, the occult, and
the art and science of love and magic. I had a vast
library at my father's home and collected thousands
of volumes of fantastic tales.*

*I learned all about ancient races and bygone
times. About myths and legends and dreams of all
people through the millennium. And the more I read
the stronger my imagination grew until I discovered
that I was able to travel into the stories… to actually
become part of them.*

*I wish I could say that I listened to my teacher
and respected my gift, as I ought to have. If I had, I
would not be telling you this tale now.
But I was foolhardy and confused, showing off
with bravery.*

*One afternoon, curious about the myth of the
Arabian Nights, I traveled back to ancient Persia to
see for myself if it was true that every day Shahryar
(Persian: شهريار, "king") married a new virgin, and then
sent yesterday's wife to be beheaded. It was written
and I had read that by the time he met Scheherazade,
the vizier's daughter, he'd killed one thousand
women.*

*Something went wrong with my efforts. I arrived
in the midst of the story and somehow exchanged
places with Scheherazade — a phenomena that had
never occurred before and that still to this day, I
cannot explain.*

*Now I am trapped in that ancient past. I have
taken on Scheherazade's life and the only way I can
protect myself and stay alive is to do what she did to
protect herself and stay alive.*

*Every night the King calls for me and listens as I spin tales.
And when the evening ends and dawn breaks, I stop at a
point that leaves him breathless and yearning for more.
And so the King spares my life for one more day, so that
he might hear the rest of my dark tale.*

*As soon as I finish a story... I begin a new
one... like the one that you, dear reader, have before
you now.*

Chapter One

Jane Hamilton did her best not to get her hopes up. It was almost sad how excited she was for the morning mail run. After all, it was her normal routine, and she'd been working on the naval base for eighteen years now, ever since her ex-husband came home one day and told her he'd met someone else and was filing for divorce.

It had cut deep. Jane had thought she'd be with Jake forever. They'd been high school sweethearts, and she'd done everything in her power to support him when he'd joined the Navy at age eighteen. But just like that, after over a decade of marriage, he'd up and left her to raise their eight-year-old daughter by herself. He'd grudgingly sent money every month (only because the courts said he had to) until she'd turned eighteen, and Jane hadn't heard from him since.

She'd gotten a contractor job on the base in the mail room, and had worked her way up over the last two decades to where she was now. She managed about ten employees and was responsible for distributing the mail throughout the base. But even though she was the boss now, she always, without fail, walked through her building, hand-delivering mail each morning. For one, it got her out of her office. She enjoyed talking to the other contractors who worked in the building and getting to know the sailors as well.

But for the last year and a half, she'd also kept up her routine because of *him*.

Storm North.

She'd literally stopped in her tracks the first time she'd seen him. He'd apparently been working at the base for a while, but had just been given an office in the same building where Jane worked. And just his name was enough to make her sigh.

Storm North.

It was so masculine, the perfect name for one of the heroes in the romance books she loved to read.

She had the worst crush on the man, which felt a little ridiculous at her age. She was fifty-one, way past the age of mindless hookups. But that didn't mean her libido was dead, and that fateful day, it had roared to life at just the sight of him. Storm was a few inches taller than her own five foot seven, but his commanding presence made his trim body seem larger than life. His close-cropped chestnut hair, distinguished silver at the temples, made his watchful hazel eyes stand out even more than they did already. Everything about him radiated strength and vitality.

He was serious most of the time, which didn't surprise her because he had a lot of responsibility. He was in charge of several SEAL teams and took his job very seriously, which she admired.

But Jane loved being able to make him smile, even if it was for just a moment as she said good morning, handed him a package, or joked about this or that.

She lived for those morning mail runs when she could see Storm.

Her daughter, Rose—whose relationship with Jane was tenuous at best—would say she was being ridiculous. That someone as important as Storm would never look twice at a lowly mail clerk such as her. Still, Jane couldn't help but fantasize about him. Fantasize that one day he'd see her, *truly* see her, and wonder why he hadn't asked her out.

But Jane didn't actually think that would ever happen. She just wasn't his type. Not that she really knew him at all, except that he used to be a SEAL himself. But she assumed he'd prefer someone beautiful, slender. He was so good-looking and in shape, and she...wasn't. Jane didn't make a habit of putting herself down, but she didn't like to work out, and she enjoyed a good glass of wine and slice of pecan pie a bit too much.

Jane had also had an extremely tough time after her divorce and was leery about getting too close to anyone again. She could be friendly and outgoing at work, but put her in a social situation and she clammed up. Storm was probably the life of the party, with no problem talking to anyone and everyone. He was genuinely nice...despite his seemingly gruff exterior.

She was sure Storm had to have a girlfriend, though he wasn't married, as far as Jane knew. She constantly checked out his left hand for a ring.

On the outside looking in, Storm North was the perfect catch, and she was…simply Jane. Plain Jane, as her ex used to call her. It was a nickname their daughter had picked up and taunted her with for most of her mean teenage years.

Raising Rose by herself hadn't been a walk in the park. At first, Jake had wanted to co-raise their daughter, but as the years went by, and he moved from one base to another, his trips to see her had become fewer and fewer. It affected Rose greatly. She'd felt abandoned, blaming her mom for the fact that her dad wasn't around. She'd snuck out of their apartment all the time in high school and graduated by the skin of her teeth.

Jane hadn't been surprised when she'd moved out on her eighteenth birthday. There were even a few years when Jane thought she'd wake up to a knock on the door from the police, letting her know that Rose was dead of an overdose or because she'd hooked up with the wrong man. But finally, after several painful years for them both, things had at least leveled out when it came to their relationship. She was twenty-six, had a steady boyfriend—who Jane didn't know at all—and was at least making an effort to be a little nicer. She wasn't sure what her daughter was doing for a living, but when Rose did reach out, she was no longer begging for money.

It was kind of pathetic that Jane was taking that as a good sign.

In the near decade that she'd been living on her own, Jane had felt as if she'd been learning who she was as a woman.

At first she'd been Jake's girlfriend. Then his Navy wife. Then she was the woman who'd been dumped and a single mother. She'd struggled for so long and so hard that she still felt as if she was finding herself. Which was somewhat silly after half a century, but there it was. And she wanted to find love again. Find a man who would support *her* as much as she supported him. Wanted someone to laugh with…and do all the naughty things she'd been fantasizing about for years and years.

But Storm North wasn't that man.

Jane knew it, but that didn't mean she could stop fantasizing about him.

Pushing the mail cart down the hallway, Jane felt her heart rate increase as she got closer to Storm's office. It was silly. Ridiculous. But she felt as if she was in middle school again, about to see the boy she had a massive crush on.

But Storm was no boy, that was for sure.

She entered his administrative assistant's office and smiled at the man sitting behind the desk.

"Good morning," she said cheerily.

"Hi, Jane," the young man replied with a smile. "Go on in. He's not in a meeting."

"Thanks," Jane told him, hoping she didn't look as excited as she felt. She didn't get to see Storm every day, since he was a very busy man, and whenever she did, it made her morning.

She picked up the small packet and three letters that had arrived for him and headed into his office. She knocked briefly and when she heard him call, "Come in," pushed open the door.

Storm was sitting behind his desk in his digitized blue battle dress uniform. She could see a bit of gray at his temples, but otherwise she'd have no idea he was in his late forties. He looked as if he could take on the young Navy SEALs he commanded any day of the week…and win.

"Good morning," Jane said softly.

Storm looked up. "Hi, Jane. How are you today?"

"I'm good. You?"

"Not so bad, now that the Admiral's Mast for one of my best SEALs is over and done with."

Jane knew what he was referring to. They might work on a huge naval base, but people talked, and word got around quickly. A SEAL named Phantom had disobeyed orders to go on leave and instead had gone to Timor-Leste to rescue a young woman. She wasn't completely sure of all the details, but what she *did* know made her romantic heart go pitter-patter.

"I'm sure that was difficult," she said diplomatically.

Storm smiled, and Jane's knees went a little weak.

"That's one word for it. So…are you doing okay? I didn't see you yesterday."

She wanted to read into that statement, feeling giddy that he'd even noticed that she wasn't there but instead shrugged nonchalantly. "I'm fine. I woke up with a migraine and took a sick day. I've got a ton of time saved up and figured I might as well use it."

"Good for you," Storm said. "I mean, being a hard worker is one thing, but never taking leave, sick, or vacation isn't healthy."

"When's the last time *you* took leave?" The question popped out before Jane could call it back.

"Touché," Storm said with an even wider smile. "I swear anytime I think about taking some time off, the shit hits the fan around here... Oh, sorry. I sometimes forget how to talk in polite company."

Jane chuckled. "Nothing you can say will surprise or offend me," she told him. "I've worked around here long enough to hear just about every swear word invented. Not to mention hearing them from my daughter when she was a teenager."

"You have a daughter?" Storm asked with a tilt of his head. "You don't look old enough to be the mother of a teenager."

Jane rolled her eyes. "Oh, please. I'm plenty old. She's twenty-six, and she gave me every one of these wrinkles on my face."

"Seriously...you look amazing. Your husband's a lucky man."

Was Storm *flirting* with her? Trying to figure out if she was married or not? Jane barely stopped herself from doing a stupid little girly dance right there in front of him. "He *was* lucky," she told him. Then added, "But he decided twenty years ago to throw me away for some young flunky. His mistake."

Storm's hazel eyes were fixed on her face, and Jane suddenly felt flustered. She'd dreamed of having his undivided attention for years, but now that she had it, she wasn't sure what to do.

"How long have you been working here?" he asked.

"Twenty years. I got the job right after he walked out."

Storm nodded. "I, for one, am grateful. I appreciate what you do. I've never had to worry about my mail getting lost, and anytime I've had an issue, it's been resolved quickly. You've trained your employees well."

That was one of the best compliments Jane had ever gotten. She wished he'd complimented her on something more personal, but she'd settle for him noticing that she was a good employee. She took great pride in running a tight ship. A lot of people didn't realize how intricate and complicated dealing with the mail could be. From packages with incomplete addresses that they had to figure out, misdelivered items, postage due...and then there was all the internal correspondence that went back and forth across the base. She and her employees were kept very busy. "Thanks," she replied with a small smile.

"That all for me this morning?" he asked with a nod toward the mail in her hand.

"Oh! Yes, sorry," Jane said, stepping forward and putting the envelopes and packet on his desk.

"No problem," Storm said. "So your head's feeling better today?" he asked.

For a second, Jane was so flustered she had no idea what he was talking about, then remembered. "Oh, yeah. Thanks. I don't get migraines a lot, but when I do, they tend to knock me off my feet. But other than a slight twinge today, I feel fine."

"Good. Then I'll see you tomorrow, right?"

Beaming, Jane nodded. "Right. Have a good day, Sir, and try not to scare newbie sailors too badly."

"It's Storm...and I'm making no promises."

Jane knew she probably looked like a big dork with the huge smile on her face, but she couldn't help it. She gave him a little finger wave and backed out of his office. When she'd cleared his door, she spun, said goodbye to his admin, and pushed her mail cart out into the hallway. She stopped outside the door and leaned against the wall, closing her eyes and sighing in contentment.

Every time she talked to Storm, she felt happy, but today was markedly different. He'd seemed more...engaged. He'd asked her about her personal life, asked for her to call him by his first name...and when he'd smiled at her, she'd gone weak in the knees.

Taking a deep breath, she continued down the hall to the next office, feeling happier than she'd felt in a very long time.

Chapter Two

Admiral Storm North sat back in his chair and stared at the doorway Jane Hamilton had just exited. He had no idea what it was about her that had caught his attention this morning. He'd talked to her frequently over the last year…but for some reason, he hadn't truly *seen* her until just now.

And he liked what he saw.

Maybe it was all his SEALs finding women of their own lately and him becoming more and more aware of his age. Maybe it was everything that had happened with Phantom and Kalee, and how hard they'd fought for their happy ending.

He didn't know. But when he'd looked up and seen Jane smiling shyly at him from his doorway, something clicked deep inside him.

Storm was happy being a workaholic. He'd enjoyed being a SEAL and doing what he could to keep his country safe. And he was thrilled to take his current position when he'd gotten too old to be an effective SEAL. Liked solving problems at work. But…

He was lonely.

Going home to his two-story townhouse, making his solitary dinner, watching TV, and going to bed by himself day in and day out was hard. He enjoyed being around people. Having no one to talk to, to share his day with, was wearing thin.

And for just a second when Jane walked in, he thought he'd recognized the same yearning for company in her eyes that he saw in his own mirror each morning. But more than that, for the first time…he saw how Jane's cheeks flushed slightly when she smiled at him. How her breathing increased slightly as they talked, how she bit her lip as if she was nervous.

All signs pointing to the fact that Jane wasn't unaffected by him.

His clumsy attempt to find out if she was married was embarrassing, but her answer was more than satisfying. Storm liked that she had enough self-esteem to say her husband *had* been lucky when they were together. He liked that she'd called him on his own lack of taking leave. One, because she could obviously think fast on her feet, and two, because it meant she was paying attention to his comings and goings.

When he'd first been moved to the building, Storm had researched all of the contractors who worked there. He liked to know who was around him and what their backgrounds were. Pulling the details about Jane from the depths of his mind wasn't hard. She'd been working as a contractor in the mail room for decades, just like she'd said. She'd worked her way up from an hourly clerk to manager. She was fifty-one, with an impeccable work record.

But chatting with her that morning had told him so much more than a piece of paper ever could. She'd been married and divorced, had a grown daughter who she obviously had a tumultuous relationship with, at least when she was a teenager. And, if he wasn't mistaken, she had more than a passing interest in him. Though he couldn't say why, for certain.

Storm knew he was good-looking. He wasn't conceited, but when he'd been active on the teams, he'd had his share of women flirt with him because of what he did or how he looked. However, since he'd retired from active missions and transitioned into his current position, he hadn't had time for women.

That didn't mean they still didn't try to reel him in. Storm couldn't count the number of wives who'd hit on him, who'd made it clear they were okay with seeing him without letting their spouses know.

Storm didn't want to sleep with a married woman. Didn't want to sneak around. He wanted a woman he could be proud to be with, who would be equally thrilled to walk by his side. And for once, he wanted to do the pursuing.

For most of his life, he hadn't had to work for a woman's attention. They came to him, and he could pick and choose which he wanted to be with. And in all honesty, it had always made him feel somewhat sleazy. The fact that Jane Hamilton had known him for quite some time and hadn't said much more than "good morning" and "hello," despite her obvious interest, intrigued him.

It had been a while since he'd had a challenge, and Storm had a feeling Jane would be more than worth the effort.

He wasn't a fall-in-love-at-first-sight guy, though, no matter that he was feeling more energized and excited about pursuing a woman than he'd felt in his entire life. So he'd take things slow. Get to know Jane over the next few weeks. Flirt with her a little and feel her out. See if he was reading things with her correctly.

Then, when the time was right and he wasn't knee deep in any projects at work, he'd ask her out. See if they had chemistry outside of the naval base.

Happy with his plan to take things slow, Storm reached for his mail and got to work.

* * * *

Jane wanted to hold on to the giddy feeling she'd gotten from talking to Storm that morning, but duty called. When she got back down to the mail room on the basement level of the building, she'd been pulled in one direction, then another. She'd been putting out fires ever since her delivery.

An admiral was upset that he hadn't received a report from someone across the base he thought he should've received that morning. Two of her employees had called in sick...one of which Jane knew she'd have to deal with and probably fire for excessive absences. And they'd received an inordinately large amount of mail that had to be sorted and delivered that afternoon. They were slammed, and Jane had no time to dissect the conversation she'd had with Storm earlier. Duty called.

Jane was helping sort the mail after lunch when a package on the conveyer belt caught her attention. At first glance, nothing about it seemed out of place. It was about half the size of a shoebox with only a little bit of tape holding it together. But when Jane looked at the way it was addressed, she realized the shipping label looked odd. There was nothing indicating who it was from, an excessive amount of postage in the corner that had clearly been canceled by hand, the box was marked "confidential," and it was addressed to Rear Admiral Creasy...except his last name was misspelled as Creasey, with an extra e.

The closer she looked, the more everything about the package screamed suspicious, and Jane had been through way too many training sessions about bombs and anthrax being sent through the mail to dismiss the package as nothing serious. If it was delivered to the rear admiral and something happened to him, Jane would never forgive herself.

Knowing she was supposed to clear the room, alert the authorities, turn off the air conditioning—just in case—and not touch or move the package until it could be examined, Jane began to set things in motion. This would delay all mail delivery for hours, possibly for an entire day, but it couldn't be helped. If this was a bomb or a biochemical agent being sent through the mail, nothing else mattered, including her timetable.

But just as Jane turned to alert everyone they had to go into lockdown protocol, one of her employees pushed a large number of boxes and envelopes down the conveyor belt toward her. The box she'd just been examining teetered on the edge of the sorting table and, acting instinctively, Jane reached out to catch it.

Everything after seemed to happen in slow motion.

The box began to fall.

Jane caught it in midair.

The jostling of the box obviously detonated something inside, because the top flew off, and an orange caustic agent sprayed into the air, covering Jane's face and arms.

She immediately began to cough and gag, but did her best to stay calm—the hardest thing she'd ever done in her life.

"Holy shit, Jane, what the hell?" one of her employees exclaimed.

"Don't touch me," she managed, her eyes squeezed tightly closed. Between coughs, she got out, "Code black. Call the naval police and initiate a code black!"

Thankfully, her employees knew exactly what to do. A code black was the highest level of emergency the mail room could declare. It meant there was some sort of chemical leak and all personnel should remove themselves from the immediate vicinity. Her office had trained for this exact scenario time and time again—but Jane had never thought she'd be contaminated.

Hearing everyone rushing out of the room, she pictured where she was in the sorting room and blindly made her way toward the wall behind her. She didn't want to touch anything, because that could spread the contaminate that was all over her hands, but with every second that passed, it got harder and harder to breathe. She had to reach the decontamination station.

Her employees had all left, as they'd been trained, and she was on her own.

Feeling as if her lungs were going to explode, Jane coughed some more, then threw up on the floor where she stood. Everything hurt, and it felt as if her face was on fire.

Falling to her knees, she tried to get oxygen into her burning lungs. For all she knew, her skin was melting off. She couldn't feel anything, couldn't make it to decontamination. The only thing she could do was kneel on the floor and retch.

* * * *

Storm was reading a report about an increase in hostilities in a small country in Africa when his admin assistant stuck his head inside his office.

"Sorry to bother you, Sir, but there's a code black in the mail room."

"Fuck. Code black? Are you sure?" he asked.

"Yes, Sir. The building's being evacuated. We need to go."

Storm surged up from his desk and headed for the door. All he could think about was the fact that Jane worked in the mail room.

It was only that morning that he'd decided to explore his interest in the shy contractor, but hearing there was some sort of biological threat in the mail room changed things drastically. Until he saw for himself that Jane was all right, he knew the feeling of concern and unease within him wouldn't abate.

Jogging down the hall, Storm headed for the stairwell. He ran down two flights and instead of exiting outside, continued down to the basement level. He passed a few people coming up the stairs, but no one dared ask him where he was going or what he was doing. His rank sometimes had its benefits.

Someone had pulled the fire alarm, and the annoying sound of the bells ringing gave him an instant headache, but he ignored it as best he could and headed for the door to the mail room. He'd only been down here a handful of times, but he knew exactly where to go.

He pulled on the door—and frowned when it didn't open. "Son of a bitch," he muttered, remembering that protocol demanded all doors be locked in case of an incident.

Standing there for a second, Storm debated what to do. It was likely Jane was standing outside right that moment with her employees, talking to the authorities and telling them what had happened. It was also likely the code black was a false alarm; there hadn't been an anthrax or sarin incident in years.

But a little part of him, deep down, thought differently.

"Jane?" he yelled, his voice barely registering above the blaring fire alarm. "Are you in there?"

He put his ear against the door and waited, straining to hear something. Anything.

"Sir?" a voice yelled from his right. "You need to exit the building."

Storm turned to see a young man standing behind him, his face as white as a sheet, wearing a pair of coveralls that indicated he worked in the mail room.

"You work in there, right?" Storm asked, ignoring his demand that he leave.

"Yes, but there's a code black. You have to go."

"What happened?" Storm barked.

The young man looked around nervously, his gaze resting on the door to the stairwell longingly. Storm did his best to calm his tone. The man was obviously scared out of his mind. "Tell me what happened. Then I'll stay until the authorities get here."

"I'm supposed to direct them here," the man said.

Impatient now, Storm said, "Talk to me."

"We were sorting the mail like usual. Jane was at the table and when a bunch of mail was pushed forward, a box fell off. She grabbed it and it exploded. She told us to initiate code black and to get out."

"Where is she?"

"Inside," the man said, and Storm could hear the tremor in his voice. "I didn't want to leave but knew she'd be pissed if I didn't. We've had drill after drill, and she always said that if anything ever happened, the last thing we should do is help the person who's infected. That the decon team will come in and do that. Do you think they're here yet?"

Fuck.

Storm had to get inside to Jane. Fuck waiting for a decontamination team. She could be dying—which was unacceptable on his watch.

Intellectually, he understood the need for isolating an infected person, but he literally couldn't stand there knowing she might be on the other side of the door suffering.

"Do you have the key?" he shouted.

The man nodded, and Storm held out his hand, wiggling his fingers in a "bring it here" motion.

Surprisingly, the man did as Storm ordered, quickly closing the gap between them and stepping up to the door. It was obvious he really *hadn't* wanted to leave Jane inside, and was clearly relieved someone was going to help her.

When the door was unlocked, Storm gestured to the stairs. "Go wait for the decon team outside and tell them where she is."

"Help her," the man said, his face drawn with concern. "She's not only a good boss, but she's a good person too. She doesn't deserve this…whatever was inside that package."

Storm nodded and pushed open the door, confident the young kid was going to get help down here as soon as he could. But he knew more than most that it would take time. No one was going to enter the building without completely suiting up to protect themselves. He didn't blame them, but as a SEAL, he wasn't one to wait around or be overly cautious.

The second he opened the door, Storm was pretty sure he knew what the bomb had contained. It wasn't an explosive, per se. It wasn't anthrax. Wasn't sarin. It smelled like CS gas. Chlorobenzylidene malononitrile. Tear gas. Pepper spray. It burned like hell when it got on you, but it wasn't lethal. Storm had been through enough training exercises with the stuff to know it *felt* as if you were dying. It burned your eyes and nose, making those orifices leak. And it made a lot of people very sick.

But it didn't kill. Thank God.

He slammed the door shut behind him, thankfully dimming the wailing of the fire alarm enough so he could hear himself think once more.

Coughing because of the residue in the air, Storm called out, "Jane? Where are you?"

He didn't hear her answer, but he did hear her coughing and gagging. He made his way around a large table—and his insides froze. Jane was on her hands and knees on the floor. A small pile of vomit was in front of her, and her eyes were squeezed shut.

Hurrying over, he hated the way she flinched violently when he grabbed her shoulders.

"It's me, Storm North," he reassured her. "Let me help you."

She shook her head and tried to wrench herself away from him. "Poison," she gasped before coughing once again.

Storm's heart lurched in his chest. She was trying to protect him.

Him. Someone she didn't know. A SEAL who'd looked death in the face more than once and survived.

Pushing down his feelings for another time, he leaned close and said urgently into her ear, "I'm pretty sure it's CS gas," he told her. "Not poison. I know it burns like hell. Did it get into your eyes?"

She nodded, and he grimaced in commiseration. In training, he'd always worn a gas mask until being told to remove it. He'd never taken a spray right in the face, and certainly never with his eyes open.

He'd been relieved when he'd opened the door to the mail room, but now he knew this was more serious than he'd first thought.

"Come on, we need to get you to the decon station."

Jane nodded and allowed him to help her to her feet, but she stayed hunched over and didn't touch him in any way, shape or form. Storm realized that was because her hands were covered with the orange-red spray, as was her upper body.

Whoever had rigged that mail bomb knew what they were doing.

In compliance with federal regulations, there was a small shower-like decontamination station in the corner of the basement mail room. As far as Storm knew, it had never been utilized...until now.

He turned on the water, and at first it came out a rusty brown color, but it quickly began to run clear. Jane whimpered at hearing the water.

Without hesitation, Storm wrapped an arm around Jane's waist and stepped under the water with her. They were both soaked in seconds, but at the moment, he didn't worry about that. He needed to wash the caustic spray off Jane's face and hands.

The water was cold, and he felt her shiver under his hands, but she didn't pull away. Snot ran down her face and she'd gotten some vomit on her clothes, both washed away in the spray, but Storm had seen far worse in battle.

Tilting her face up to the water, Jane did her best to not drown herself as she tried to wash off the spray and cough at the same time.

Storm wasn't unaffected by the toxic atmosphere, although he hadn't gotten a direct hit in the face. He felt his eyes watering and his own mucus membranes doing their best to repel the nasty chemical. But he ignored his own suffering and concentrated on doing what he could for Jane.

Her medium length brown hair was covered in the CS gas, and he tried to help her wash it out. Everywhere he looked, he saw the telltale signs of the orange spray. "You're going to have to take off your shirt and pants," he told her as gently as he could. "I can see it dripping down your body."

For just a moment she seemed to panic, but then she wiped her face of all emotion. She hadn't opened her eyes longer than it took to try to rinse them out, but he felt her body tense under his hands.

Finally, she nodded and brought her hands up to the first button on her shirt.

"I've got it," Storm told her.

It suddenly felt as if they were the only two people in the world, the situation more intimate than it should have been, given the circumstances. Storm quickly undid the buttons on her shirt one by one, helping her shrug out of it when he was done. She was left standing in front of him in a soaking white cotton bra that did nothing to hide her assets. She was full figured and rounded in all the right places. Her nipples were taut from the cold water, and he saw goose bumps on her arms.

"Hang on, almost done," he soothed, reaching for the belt around her waist. He quickly undid it and unbuttoned her khakis. He circled her and kneeled, pulling the wet material down. She kicked off her shoes and stepped out of her pants.

Storm stood and pushed her clothes off to the side. He moved until he was standing in front of her again, but not in the way of the shower. He put his hands on either side of her face and gently tilted it up into the water. "You're going to have to try to keep your eyes open as long as you can, Jane. I know it hurts, but you have to wash that shit out."

She nodded, coughed, then squinted, doing her best to follow his directions. Storm could see how much it hurt, and he couldn't help but admire her bravery. "That's it. Good. Just like that."

He had no idea how long they'd stood in the cramped decontamination shower, but eventually she was able to keep her eyes open for longer than half a second at a time. They were bloodshot and red rimmed when she finally opened them long enough to look at him, and when she did, he hated what he saw there.

Shame. Embarrassment.

"I'm sorry," she whispered, then coughed violently once more.

"You have nothing to be sorry about," he told her vehemently. "*Nothing*. From where I'm standing, you did everything right."

"I couldn't get to the decon station," she admitted. "Everything hurt too bad. I fucked up."

Storm was shaking his head before she'd finished speaking. "No, you did what you were trained to do. You got your employees out, did what you could to keep the particulates from escaping."

"I threw up," she whispered.

Storm hated the embarrassment she so obviously felt. "That's your body's way of getting rid of whatever is contaminating it. It's nothing to be ashamed of, Jane. You should see the cadets in boot camp. They act like they're dying, and they don't get nearly as big a dose of CS gas in their faces as you did."

"You're *sure* it was CS gas?" she asked.

"Ninety-nine percent, yeah," Storm told her. "I recognized the smell the second I walked into the room."

She frowned. "How'd you get in here?"

"One of your employees in the hall let me in."

"He was supposed to—"

Whatever she was going to say got cut off midsentence when the door to the mail room opened, and three men wearing full decontamination suits were standing there. The clear shower curtain was the only thing separating her and Storm from the rest of the room.

"Oh shit," she said, then coughed even as she hunched her shoulders inward, trying to hide herself from them.

Without thought, Storm pulled her into his body, something inside him softening when he felt her melt against him, as if she were invisible to the newcomers simply by standing in his arms.

One of the men had a device in his hand that would measure the air for contaminates. It would tell him what materials they were dealing with, and the percentages. The other two held what looked like long-handled brushes.

Storm stiffened and turned sideways, trying to shield Jane from their eyes.

"Step away from her, Sir," one of the men said, his voice muffled from the head-to-toe protection suit he was wearing.

"Not a chance," Storm retorted fiercely, ruining his command with a hard, hacking cough.

"Sir, you both need to be decontaminated before we can get you to medical."

Storm knew the protocol. Hell, he'd help write the damn manual once upon a time, but back then it had seemed very clinical. Scrubbing down a contaminated person so they didn't spread particulates to innocents in a hospital setting was the right thing to do. But holding a shivering and traumatized Jane in his arms made it very clear that being hosed down and scrubbed as if she were a dirty piece of flesh wasn't exactly ethical or humane.

Fuck.

He tightened his arms around her just before she took a deep breath and pulled away from him. "It's all right," she said quietly. She was squinting, and it was obviously still painful for her to open her eyes. "It's protocol."

She was right, but that didn't make it any easier to let her go.

He watched as Jane bravely stepped out of the decon shower and held her arms out from her sides. Her white underwear was completely soaked and see-through from the back. Storm could only imagine what she looked like from the front.

His teeth clenched, and he wanted to pound the seaman holding the scrubber.

But instead, he did the only thing he could to make Jane feel less awkward in that moment. He stripped off his own clothes until he stood next to her wearing nothing but his own pair of white underwear.

Chapter Three

Jane wanted to die. Hours earlier, she'd been giddy about her conversation with Storm, and now she wanted to sink into the ground and disappear. Knowing he'd been the one who'd found her on her hands and knees, puking her guts out and covered in CS gas, was already embarrassing as hell. And if that wasn't enough, he'd stripped off her clothes and seen her in all her fifty-one-year-old glory.

She didn't expect herself to look like she had at twenty, but she wasn't sure being practically naked in front of the man she'd been crushing on before they'd even enjoyed more than small talk was the way to catch his attention. And she certainly didn't want to be scrubbed down like she was in a car wash, but protocol was protocol.

She'd almost had a heart attack when she'd looked to her left and saw Storm standing next to her in nothing but his underwear. He'd given her a lopsided smile and shrugged...and something inside her had melted in that moment. He didn't have to strip, and they'd both known that. He wasn't there when the box had exploded, and any pepper spray on him was secondary transfer from her own clothes and hands. But he'd done it anyway.

That right there had been enough to earn her loyalty and undying support from here to eternity.

Now she was sitting in the medical clinic on base, wrapped in a huge blanket and wearing a pair of scrubs someone had scrounged up for her, waiting to be discharged.

Her eyes still burned, and she hadn't been able to stop coughing, but at least she didn't feel as if she were going to bring up her lungs with every cough anymore.

Naval Criminal Investigative Services was looking into the package and trying to figure out who'd sent it. Rear Admiral Creasy and his wife had been alerted that he'd been the target of a mail bomb, and they were taking precautions until the sender could be identified and apprehended.

The mail room was under quarantine until further notice, and Jane knew she'd have a ton of extra work to do to get things up and running in the temporary room they'd been given. She was extremely proud of her staff for acting immediately and doing exactly what they were trained to do. Namely, leaving her in the room and going to get help. The last thing anyone wanted was for a contaminant to spread and hurt or kill more people. This time the bomb only held pepper spray, but next time it could be anthrax or sarin.

If she was being honest with herself...she was lucky. Still, everything about the last few hours had sucked. She literally thought that was it, she was dead. When the box exploded, she'd had a split second to regret all the things she hadn't done in her life, and some of the things she had. Then, instead of dying, when she'd fallen to the ground in the most pain she'd ever felt in her life and couldn't breathe, she'd *wished* she was dead.

And to make things worse, the man she admired more than anyone in the world, who she wanted to impress, had come in when she had snot running down her face and a pile of vomit in front of her and couldn't do anything to help herself.

But...Storm had been amazing. Strong when she'd been weak. He'd taken over and done what needed to be done. It had been a very long time since she'd been able to rely on anyone. The only thing she'd had to think about when Storm had arrived was doing exactly as he said. She'd felt safe in his arms, and even though it had hurt like hell to open her eyes, she'd done it when he'd ordered her to, grateful to see him.

Of course, wishing she was about thirty pounds lighter now was useless, given the fact that she'd been almost naked in front of him. But she couldn't be too upset when she recalled the look in his eyes when she'd last seen him. Respect and admiration.

Or she could've just been delirious and it was actually pity.

Closing her eyes—because it still felt better than having them open—Jane put her head on the back of the chair she was sitting in and prayed the doctors would hurry up with her discharge papers.

The minutes inched by slowly. Her head hurt. All she wanted to do was go home and take another shower—she didn't think she'd ever feel clean again—and sleep. She was exhausted and didn't want to think about anything anymore.

Her stomach growled, but she ignored it. She'd attempt an apple or something when she got home, but truthfully, the thought of eating turned her stomach.

"Hey."

The one word was said softly, but she still startled badly.

Eyes flying open, Jane stared at Admiral Storm North. He was leaning against the doorjamb of her room, staring at her. She had no idea how long he'd been standing there, but she had the feeling it had been a while.

"Hi," she croaked. Her throat was scratchy from all the coughing, sounding funny to her own ears.

Storm frowned. "What are you still doing here?"

"I'm waiting to be discharged."

He looked at his watch. "It's eight-thirty."

Jane raised an eyebrow. "I know."

"Damn," he muttered. "I'll be right back."

Too tired to care where he was going, Jane closed her eyes again and rested her head on the back of the chair once more.

It could've been five minutes or an hour when Storm returned. "The doctor should be here with your discharge papers in a minute or two."

Jane opened her eyes and looked at him. "What'd you do, threaten to court-martial him?"

When Storm didn't even crack a smile, Jane frowned. "You didn't...did you?"

"No," he said, coming toward her. He squatted in front of her chair and stared into her eyes. "How're you feeling?" he asked quietly.

Jane shrugged. "I'm okay."

He frowned at her answer. "How about you try that again...and be honest this time?"

Jane sighed. "I'm okay, Sir. A little tired, my head hurts, and my eyes still sting a bit, but I'll be fine in the morning."

"I told you to call me Storm," he told her.

Jane licked her lips. She saw his eyes dart down to her mouth, then back up to meet her gaze once more. She couldn't read the look in his eyes. "I'm not sure that's appropriate."

"You don't work for me. You aren't even in the Navy. And after what we went through today, I'd say it's more than appropriate."

Jane couldn't argue that. "I haven't thanked you, have I?" she asked.

Storm shook his head. "No need."

She snorted. "I'd say there is."

Then he shocked the shit out of her by bringing his hand up and palming the side of her neck. His thumb brushed against the underside of her jaw lightly as he said, "How have I known you for so long without ever really seeing you?"

The question was said softly, and Jane wasn't sure if he really wanted her to answer or if he was talking to himself. Either way, goose bumps broke out on her arms.

"I'm glad I was there," he went on. "When I heard something had happened in the mail room, I couldn't even think about evacuating the building."

"Why?" Jane whispered.

"Because I just knew you'd be down there, working to contain whatever happened, and that you might need help."

"That wasn't smart," she scolded. "If that had been anthrax or something worse, you would've gotten hurt as well."

"But it wasn't, and you *did* need help," he said easily. "And I couldn't *not* go. I can't explain it. I suddenly feel as if I've known you forever, but at the same time I know next to nothing. I had decided after our talk this morning to take things slow. Get to know you better. Maybe ask you out after a month or so. You're funny. Beautiful. Smart. Independent. All traits that I admire and respect.

"What happened today feels like someone smacking me upside the back of my head and telling me to get my shit together. I, more than most, know how short life can be. I'm normally a go-after-what-I-want kind of guy, but I thought I should go slow with you. I mean, why would you think I was seriously interested if, after knowing you for so long, I suddenly asked you out? So I'd decided to wait. But...fuck that."

Jane stared at Storm with huge eyes. Was he serious? He couldn't be.

"Want to go out to dinner tomorrow night?"

"With you?" she blurted.

He chuckled. "Yeah. With me."

She opened her mouth to say not only yes, but hell yes, when the doctor chose that moment to enter.

Storm stood but didn't leave the room.

"Sorry about the delay. I've signed your papers and you can head home. If your eyes continue to burn after another eight hours, please come back, and we'll check you out again. And I'm serious about that. Don't think it'll just go away. CS gas is caustic, and you took a direct hit to the face. You could lose your eyesight if you don't take it seriously."

Jane nodded at the doctor. "I will."

"And you should rinse them out at least every three hours tonight. Set an alarm to get up and do it. Don't go home and fall asleep and forget. It's important, Ms. Hamilton. Do you have someone who can make sure you get home all right?"

Jane opened her mouth to tell the doctor that she was a grown-ass woman and could manage to get a taxi and get herself home, but Storm beat her to it.

"I'm taking her home."

"Great." The doctor turned to the admiral and handed over her discharge papers, explaining in detail what she should be watching for in the next twenty-four hours. "Any questions or concerns?"

The question was aimed at Storm, which annoyed her. To his credit, though, Storm looked at her and raised an eyebrow. She shook her head, just wanting to go home instead of getting into an argument about misogyny.

"Okay. Again, come back if you start feeling more pain or have other symptoms. I'm very glad you're all right, Ms. Hamilton. People who send mail bombs are cowards, and it's a relief no one got hurt worse." And with that, the doctor, turned and left the room.

Jane scowled when the door shut behind him.

Storm held up a hand. "Before you rip me a new asshole, I had nothing to do with that. And I agree that it was sexist and annoying. He should've been talking to you, not me."

Jane's anger deflated instantly. "I hate that," she said. "I mean, I've been working on this base for a very long time, you'd think I'd be used to being talked down to, but I'm not. I'm perfectly able to take care of myself, and it's rude as hell for him to essentially pat me on the head and talk to you instead of me."

"I agree. You ready to go?"

Jane took a deep breath. She could continue to rail at the sexism, not to mention unprofessionalism, of the doctor, but she couldn't fault his expertise. He'd also been as gentle as possible when he'd cleaned out her eyes and examined her. "I'm ready," she said. "But you don't have to take me home, Storm. I'm a big girl, I can get there by myself."

"I know, but your apartment's on my way. It's not a big deal."

Jane stood, giving him side-eye. "How do you know where I live?"

She could've sworn she saw Storm blush. "I…uh…looked it up before I headed over here. If you were still here, I figured you might need a ride."

Jane couldn't help but smile. "Fine. You can take me home."

As they walked out of the room, Storm said, "You're a hard woman to do a favor for."

Jane shrugged. "I've been on my own a long time. Had to do everything myself. Learned the hard way that relying on someone else brought me nothing but heartbreak."

Storm looked at her as they passed through the waiting room at the clinic. "I'm sorry."

"Don't be. I've had a long time to get over my ex. What's that line from *Shawshank Redemption?* Get busy livin' or get busy dyin'. I chose to live."

Then Storm shocked her for the second time in minutes by reaching out and taking her hand in his. He did it so smoothly that it felt completely natural and not awkward in the least. "Some birds aren't meant to be caged," he said quietly as they headed outside and toward the parking area. "When they fly away, the part of you that knows it was a sin to lock them up rejoices, but still, the place you live in is that much more gray after they're gone."

Jane stopped in her tracks, and since he was holding her hand, Storm stopped too. "That was from *Shawshank* too," she told him unnecessarily.

"It was. Best fucking movie ever. I've watched it at least a hundred times, and every time I'm flicking through the channels and see that it's on, I have to stop. That part where Red is narrating how Andy Dufresne crawled through five hundred yards of shit and came out clean on the other side gets me every time," Storm said.

Jane nodded. "Most people don't think it's a very uplifting movie, but I can't help but think about how much Andy changed everyone's lives in that prison." Then she blushed. "I mean…I know it's fiction, but—"

"I know what you mean," Storm assured her. Then he squeezed her hand. "Come on, let's get you home. You've got to be tired."

And without a word, Jane let him lead her to his car, a navy-blue four-door VW Golf. When they were inside headed toward the exit of the base, she couldn't help but tease him. "A Golf?" she asked.

Storm chuckled. "I know, but she's got a two hundred ninety-two-horsepower engine in her that matches the power of a Ford Mustang. I like staying under the radar but having the ability to get the job done when it counts."

Jane stared at him for a second, then bit her lip trying not to laugh. But it was no use. She burst out laughing at the serious look on his face.

He glanced over at her in surprise, then grinned. When she had herself under control, he said wryly, "Didn't mean that the way it sounded."

"I guessed," Jane told him.

"You should do that more often," Storm said.

"What?"

"Laugh."

Self-conscious now, Jane looked away, turning to stare out the window.

"Shit, sorry. It was a compliment. I loved that even after the shittiest day ever, you could still find something to laugh about. Your smile lights up your face and makes you even more beautiful than you already are."

Jane turned again to look back at Storm. Her head was spinning at how he'd gone from being one of the men she delivered mail to each day to someone who had asked her out and was now going out of his way to flirt with her. It was as confusing as it was flattering and exciting. But Jane wasn't about to throw herself headlong into a relationship with *anyone*...she was too jaded for that.

"You're confusing me," she admitted softly.

"How so?" he asked without hesitation.

"Twelve hours ago you didn't know I existed. And now..." Her voice trailed off.

Storm winced. "I'm coming on too strong. I know, I'm sorry. Here's the thing...I've always been the kind of man who keeps my head down and gets the job done. I was that way as a SEAL, and I'm that way as a commander. I tend to focus on one thing at a time, and that's not always a good thing. I've known *of* you for a while, but never really took the time to *get* to know you.

"This morning, I realized that I'd been an idiot. That you've been right in front of my face the whole time, but I was too busy looking down, getting the job done. I couldn't see the forest for the trees. I'd already decided to change that. To get to know you even better, and then that damn CS bomb happened. It was a massive wake-up call. And I'm a very determined man, Jane."

"I'm not a mission," she gently chided. "You can't just decide you want me and expect to get me."

Amazingly, his cheeks flushed. "I know, and I'm saying this all wrong. I'm still willing to take things slow, but I'm letting you know up front what my intentions are."

"And what *are* your intentions?" Jane asked. "I'm not interested in anything casual," she told him. "But I'm not necessarily looking for another husband either. Tried that, it didn't work out. I'm too old to go out to bars to pick up men, and honestly…I don't *need* a man."

"But do you want one?" Storm asked quietly.

Jane blinked in surprise.

"I'm asking because the older I get, the more I realize how lonely I've become. I love my job and what I do, but when I'm lying in my bed at night, alone, I wonder what it'd be like to have someone to share my life with. I'm well aware that time is passing, and with each tick of the clock, my life is getting shorter. Eventually I'll have to retire, and spending the rest of my days with only myself for company isn't something I'm looking forward to."

This was a very deep conversation, but Jane couldn't help but be drawn to Storm even more for being honest. "When I got divorced, I thought I'd find someone else and remarry. But as time went by, and as I struggled with raising my daughter, eventually I became resigned to the fact that I'd be alone the rest of my life. But to answer your earlier question…I'm not opposed to finding a man I can love again. Someone who respects me and doesn't expect me to be someone I'm not. I'd like someone who shares some of my interests, so we have something to talk about when we're old and gray. Well…older and grayer."

"Like *Shawshank Redemption*?" Storm asked.

"Yes," Jane said quietly. With a start, she realized that they'd arrived at her apartment complex.

Storm pulled up at the entrance and turned to look at her. "Are you going in to work tomorrow?" he asked.

Jane nodded. "Yeah. Things are going to be insane. I doubt the mail room will be cleared yet, but the mail doesn't stop. We'll need to sort everything by hand. Not to mention deal with upset customers whose stuff is stuck in limbo in the mail room. I have to be there."

"I figured that's what you'd say."

Jane mentally gave him brownie points for not insisting she stay home and rest.

"I know we usually get to work around the same time in the morning. I've seen you pull into the parking lot more than once. Since your car is still on base, I'd be happy to swing by here and pick you up tomorrow...if you haven't made other arrangements."

Jane's first inclination was to decline. To say that it was an imposition for him to pick her up. That she could call a taxi.

Then she reconsidered. She'd been half in love with this man for months. She'd be an idiot not to take him up on his offer. He might turn out to be a jerk, but at least she'd know and could get rid of her stupid crush.

But what if he wasn't? What if he was as amazing as he seemed to be?

"I'd appreciate that," she told him finally.

He smiled. "Good. For a second, I thought you might refuse me. Then I'd have to go home and lick my wounds and figure out another way to spend some time with you."

"Well, you did ask me out to dinner tomorrow," Jane blurted, then immediately regretted it. Shit, maybe he'd forgotten about that, or even changed his mind.

"I did. But you haven't answered yet."

"I don't like seafood," she said. "I mean, I know we live near the coast, but I've never acquired a taste for it."

"Noted," Storm said easily. "I'll be sure to pick a place that has a variety of things to choose from. I'm not into fancy restaurants," he said. "Especially not on first dates."

"That's fine with me. I'm more of an Olive Garden kind of girl than a Ruth's Chris."

"So it's a date?" he asked.

Jane nodded.

His gaze bored into her own. "You won't regret it. I won't let you down, Jane," he said seriously.

"I hope not," she replied. "Although I should warn you, I've had a crush on you forever, so you've got a lot to live up to."

She couldn't believe she'd admitted that, though she also couldn't deny something about Storm made her feel completely at ease.

Jane loved the glimpse of the small dimple in his cheek when he smiled. "I'll do my best to live up to your expectations." Then he lifted a hand and brushed a strand of hair behind her ear. His skin was warm, and she wanted nothing more than to tilt her head into his hand, but she refrained.

"Thank you for helping me today," she told him. "I don't know what I would've done if you hadn't shown up."

"I have no doubt whatsoever you would've made your way to the decon station and gotten yourself straightened out," he said.

Jane wasn't so sure about that, but it felt good that he had confidence in her. "I hope seeing me almost naked didn't scar you for life." She had no idea why she'd said such a thing. She'd decided earlier to pretend the nakedness had never happened. That Storm North hadn't stripped her and held her close under the shower spray. But her mouth had an alarming habit of running away from her around this man.

His thumb brushed against the apple of her cheek as he said, "In the moment, I wasn't thinking about anything other than washing that shit off of you so you could breathe again. I was in SEAL mode. But afterward, when I knew you were going to be all right, I couldn't help but stare at you standing in front of me, soaking wet, wearing nothing but your underwear…and I have to say, I can't remember anyone who's turned me on more."

Reminding herself that she was a mature woman, and not a blushing teenager, Jane said, "I'm not exactly young…and have the body to prove it."

"Neither am I," he countered. "And trust me…you've got a body made for lovin'. Your curves go on for days, and I'd consider myself a lucky man if you decided to share yourself with me in the future."

She liked how he put that. "You aren't too shabby yourself," Jane felt compelled to say. "And you totally didn't have to strip down, but…I appreciated it."

They stared at each other for a long moment. Jane had no idea what he was thinking, but she loved the look of adoration she thought she saw in his eyes as he watched her.

"I should give you my number in case you need something overnight. If your eyes get worse or something."

Jane nodded. "Okay." She pulled her phone out of her purse, which had been brought to her by an officer, and programmed his number in when he recited it to her. Then she sent him a quick text. "There, now you have mine too."

"Don't forget to set your alarm to get up every few hours to rinse out your eyes," Storm reminded her.

"I won't."

"If you feel sick or something seems off, don't hesitate to call. I can take you back to the clinic."

"I'll be fine," Jane told him.

"Even so," he insisted.

"Okay, I'll let you know."

"See you in the morning," Storm said.

Jane nodded and reached for the door handle. She climbed out, then stood awkwardly on the sidewalk in front of her apartment complex for a moment. She wasn't in the least offended he hadn't opened her door or walked her into the building. It was late, he'd gone out of his way to drive her home. She wasn't about to put him out even more by making him park and walk her inside when she'd been doing it on her own for the last two decades.

But that didn't mean she didn't get all the feels when she turned around at the door to her building and saw that he hadn't pulled away from the curb yet. That he was watching to make sure she made it inside safely.

She waved at him, and he gave her a chin lift in return. Only when she opened the door and went inside did he finally pull away from the curb and head home.

It felt good to take a shower in her own bathroom and use her own soap. She rinsed her eyes out once more, only wincing a little at the pain this time, and got ready for bed. Ignoring the way her stomach growled, Jane snuggled under her covers and clutched one of the eight pillows she kept on her bed to her chest.

The day had started like any other, then taken a horrible turn, but now, Jane felt almost giddy about tomorrow. She'd be slammed at work and would likely have to answer the same questions about how she was doing over and over, but nothing could dim her excitement.

Somehow, she'd scored a date with *the* Storm North. Her expectations might not match the fantasies she'd had about him for so long, but she wasn't going to worry about that. She was going to enjoy the ride for as long as she was on it.

Chapter Four

Storm pulled up to Jane's apartment at five thirty-two the next morning. One of the things he admired about Jane was her work ethic. She wasn't afraid to work hard, and that went a long way with him. He'd worked his ass off for so long—showing up early to formation, working overtime without complaint—that it was second nature to him. Too many times he'd dated women who'd complained about how early he left for work and how late he stayed in the afternoons. He had a feeling Jane wouldn't ever bitch about that. In fact, he had a feeling he'd be the one wishing she worked a little less so she could spend more time with *him*.

Storm loved his job, but as he'd told Jane the day before, he knew his time as an officer was coming to an end. He'd had an amazing career with the Navy, but he couldn't work forever. And he wanted to enjoy his retirement. And seeing Rocco and his team, as well as Wolf and *his* team, all happily married and making their relationships work made him yearn for the same. Things with Jane might not work out, but he was at least open to a relationship.

He pulled out his phone to text her, to let her know he was there, but it wasn't necessary. He saw her exiting her building and coming toward him. After she opened the car door and sat down, he eyed her critically for a moment.

"Hi," she said cheerily.

That was another thing he liked about her. She was almost always in a good mood. At least she seemed to be at work. She made him happier just by being around her. "Hi," he returned. "You look like you're feeling better. Your eyes aren't as bloodshot."

"I am. I followed the doctor's orders and got up every two or three hours to wash them out. I might be a zombie by the end of the day though. I like my sleep," she said with a small smile.

Storm frowned. "We can postpone dinner if you're too tired."

"Oh, no, I wasn't...I didn't mean to imply...shoot," she said with a wrinkle of her nose. "I'm good, Storm. Promise. There were nights when Rose was a teenager I didn't get *any* sleep, and I still managed to make it through my shift. I'm okay."

The more glimpses Jane gave him of her life, the more Storm wanted to know. "You've mentioned several times that your daughter was a handful," he said, letting his voice trail off as he pulled out onto the road that led toward the base.

"That's putting it mildly," Jane told him. "It wasn't an easy time, that's for sure. She rebelled against every rule I gave her, blamed me for her dad leaving, and basically hated me for her entire high school career. She thought I was stifling her and didn't want her to have any fun, when in reality she was dating losers who did their best to drag her down into the world of drugs." Jane shook her head. "I had looked forward to having a close friendship with my daughter. To watching her play the flute in the marching band and being proud when she earned a spot in the National Honor Society...and instead I spent most of my time browbeating her to go to school and physically sitting outside her door, making sure she didn't sneak out in the middle of the night."

"Damn, I'm sorry," Storm said.

Jane shrugged. "I love Rose, but there were times I hated her...if that makes sense."

"It does. How's your relationship now?" he asked.

"It's okay. We're never going to be best friends, which sucks, but she calls me every now and then, and we manage to have a good conversation."

"That's good," Storm told her.

"Yeah. You ever been married?" Jane asked.

"Nope. And before you ask, no kids either. I dated quite a bit when I was a SEAL, but it never seemed fair to tie someone to me permanently. I was gone a lot, and honestly, I put all my energy toward my job. I wouldn't have been a good husband."

"And that's changed now?"

Storm respected her for asking. "Yeah, it has. Because I'm no longer active on the teams, I'm home every night. Well, almost every night. I love what I do, and I take the safety of the men on my teams seriously. But I don't live and breathe missions as I once did. I'm not saying I'll be a perfect husband or catch, but I've learned a lot over the years. Not to mention I've got some pretty damn good role models around me. Rear Admiral Creasy is one of my mentors. He's been married to Brenae for years, and they're just as in love today as they were when they met. I admire that."

"I'm sure it hasn't been easy," Jane mused.

"Of course not. She's been through hell, but she's never given up on him, and Dag goes out of his way to make sure his wife is happy and safe."

"That was the opposite of my marriage," Jane said.

Storm was thrilled she was opening up to him. He appreciated that they weren't talking about superficial topics like the weather. He craved getting to know Jane better, and this was exactly what he wondered about...what made her tick.

"How's that?" he asked when she didn't continue.

"Jake stopped trying. I was at home waiting for him with our kid, and he was off having fun and basically didn't feel as if he had any responsibilities. He'd get home, and I'd go off on him for leaving me alone and for not helping me more. The more I bitched, the more he pulled away. Until eventually he found someone who was more fun, wasn't such a downer."

"That's bullshit," Storm told her. "Having a child is a huge responsibility. He should've known that going in. And it takes two people to make a relationship work. If he wasn't helping you or making you feel appreciated, that's on him, not you."

"I guess," Jane said. "Anyway, it doesn't matter. Do I wish things were different? Yes and no. Yes, because that might've made Rose happier, made her teenage years less difficult. No, because I've learned to be a strong woman as a result of him leaving. I don't think I'd have the career I do if we were still together, and I definitely wouldn't be as confident in myself."

Storm admired Jane. She was able to find the good in a situation that was anything but. "You're amazing," he said quietly. Glancing over at her, he saw she was blushing. It was adorable.

"I'm not. I'm just me. Have you heard anything about who sent that package?" she asked.

Realizing that he'd made her uncomfortable, Storm made a mental note to compliment her as often as possible in the future, to hopefully make her truly believe how wonderful she was and not think he was blowing smoke up her ass. "Not yet. NCIS is doing what they can to track it down. The info you gave them about the packaging and the address will definitely help, though."

"I can't imagine anyone having it out for the rear admiral. Granted, I don't know him except in a work capacity, but from what I do know, he's always been nothing but respectful and kind."

"He is," Storm agreed. "But he's also had to make some tough decisions when it comes to staffing and missions. And that can make enemies."

"You think it's someone who worked for him?" she asked.

"I think it's too early at this point to know for sure. But generally people who send shit like that in the mail are cowards and afraid to confront someone face-to-face. It could also be someone who doesn't have access to the base, so they had to resort to the mail."

"I didn't think about that," Jane said worriedly. "Do you think he's safe? Someone might come after him at his house."

Storm reached out and took her hand in his. He'd held her hand the day before, and it had felt so right. So normal. He wasn't a touchy-feely kind of person, so even he was surprised he'd reached for her again, but the second her fingers closed around his, a jolt went through his body, and he couldn't bear to let go of her. "Dag is always careful. He'll be on the lookout for anything unusual."

"Good."

"Which reminds me…once the press gets ahold of the story, things are going to be hectic for you."

"Yeah, I figured as much," Jane said with a shrug. "They'll want to know all the gritty details and they'll get up in my face about it for a few days, but then some political figure will do or say something stupid and they'll forget about me."

"Just be careful, okay?"

"I will. Luckily, they can't get to me on base, so I'll just hide out at work like usual, and eventually they'll get sick of staking out my apartment."

Storm frowned, not liking the thought of her having to fight the paparazzi just to get home. But since she didn't seem overly worried, he didn't want to make a big deal out of it. "If you want an escort, let me know."

"Thanks. But I think you've carted my ass around enough for a few days."

They were nearing the gates to the base, and Storm took the ID that Jane dug out of her purse. He handed it, along with his own military ID, over to the guards, nodding when they were returned, and they were allowed to proceed. He searched his head for something else to talk about and mentally berated himself when nothing came to mind. He was out of practice in talking to women, and he hated it.

He pulled up next to the only other car in the parking lot of their building, which he knew was Jane's, and shut off the engine. "Don't overdo it today," he said gently.

She gave him a small smile. "I can't guarantee that."

"I know. You're a lot like me. But a word of caution, I was shot once on a mission and refused to follow my doctor's orders and went back to work before I should've. Ended up missing an extra week and a half because my wound got infected and I was knocked on my ass as a result."

"I wasn't shot," Jane said softly. "I'm okay."

"I know, but CS gas isn't exactly fun. And you got a face full of it. Just take it easy, okay?"

She nodded. Then after a few seconds said, "It's weird."

"What's weird?" Storm asked when she didn't elaborate.

"Having someone be concerned. I mean, I've been on my own for so long, coped with whatever life has thrown my way by myself, that it's just a bit odd to have someone else be interested in my well-being."

"I'm interested," Storm reassured her. "I know we're still getting to know each other, but I wouldn't have asked you out if I didn't want to see where things between us can go. And I can't get to know you if you drop dead in the middle of the workday, can I?"

He loved it when Jane laughed. "True."

How he'd missed "seeing" her for so long was beyond him. Now that he had, he couldn't seem to take his eyes, or his thoughts, from her.

"Come on, if we sit out here much longer, someone will wonder what we're doing," she said.

"We could give them something to wonder about," Storm suggested before he could stop himself.

It took a second for her to react, but then she laughed again. "I don't kiss on the first date," she told him with a wink. "But maybe tomorrow."

With every word out of her mouth, Storm liked her more and more. He figured she was also warning him not to expect anything after their date tonight, which was smart of her, and fine with him. He was enjoying their courtship...even if it had only been a day.

"I like you, Jane Hamilton," he blurted.

She blushed and said quietly, "I like you too, Storm North."

Then they both got out of his car and walked side by side into the building to get to work.

* * * *

Work had sucked.

But it wasn't the first time, and it wouldn't be the last.

Jane was busy from the second she'd walked into the room they'd been given to use for the day until the second she'd walked out at five in the afternoon. Normally she'd work late, trying to get caught up, but her head hurt...and she had a date to get ready for.

Storm had texted her a few hours ago to make sure they were still on, and she didn't have the heart to tell him no. Besides, she wanted to go to dinner with him. Wanted to get to know him better. The more time she spent with him, the more time she *wanted* to spend. He could definitely break her heart, way more than Jake had. But nothing ventured, nothing gained. And this was *Storm*. The man she'd lusted after for what felt like forever. She wasn't going to say no.

The mail room should be ready for them to go back to tomorrow. NCIS had concluded their investigation today, and it had been cleaned from top to bottom to clear out the lingering stench of the CS gas. Jane was more than ready to get back to normal, even if they'd be on high alert for quite a while, watching to see if there were any more bombs delivered to the base.

But for now, Jane was looking forward to her date. It had been way too long since she'd been on one, and as she stood in front of her closet, she wondered what the hell she should wear. She didn't want to look like she was trying too hard, but then again, she didn't want to look like she didn't care either.

In the end, she decided on her favorite pair of jeans and a long-sleeve black V-neck top with her shoulders showing. It made her feel sexy and confident and not over or underdressed. She had no idea where Storm was taking her for dinner, but she figured she couldn't go wrong with what she had on no matter where they ended up.

Storm had offered to pick her up, and even though she felt bad he'd been driving her all over the place recently, she'd agreed.

She wasn't surprised when he knocked on her door five minutes early. She was always early, no matter where she went, and liked that he seemed to be the same.

"Hi," she said as she opened her door. "I'm ready, I just need to grab my purse."

"You look beautiful," Storm said as he eyed her from head to toe.

Jane knew she was blushing but didn't care. "You do too. I mean, look handsome, that is." And he did. He also had on a pair of jeans, which clung to his muscular thighs. She was used to seeing him in his uniform, and there was just something extremely sexy about seeing him "dressed down" in denim. He was wearing a light blue polo shirt that seemed to make his hazel eyes look even brighter.

He took a step toward her and put his hand on her waist and leaned in. He briefly kissed her on the cheek before pulling back.

"You smell good," she blurted, then wrinkled her nose.

But he simply smiled. "Thanks. I worked out with one of my teams this afternoon and didn't think you'd want to be anywhere near me with the way I smelled, so I had to shower before I came over."

"I appreciate it," she teased. "I mean, some girls might like the au natural smell, but I'm not one of them."

"So noted," he said. "And you smell good yourself."

"Thanks. It's my lotion."

They stood in the entryway to her apartment staring at each other for a long moment before she said, "I should get my purse so we can go."

Only then did Storm take a step back. As Jane fetched her purse, she couldn't help but think about how thrilling their chemistry was. It also seemed as if, once he'd decided to pursue her, he was one hundred percent in. He was intense and focused, and it felt good to be on the receiving end of his attention.

And somehow she had a feeling the crush she'd had on him for so long was nothing compared to how much she could come to care for him. If she felt this pull toward him after only a day, she had no idea how powerful the feeling would become if they continued to date.

Shaking her head and deciding to just enjoy the moment, Jane grabbed her purse and headed back to where she'd left Storm. Like a gentleman, he hadn't come farther into her apartment and was still waiting at her door. It was warm enough outside that she didn't need a jacket or sweater since she wore a long-sleeve shirt, and so they both exited her place and she locked the door behind them.

Storm took hold of her hand as he led her to the elevator, and she couldn't help but feel all tingly inside at the contact. When they were inside his car and on their way, she broke the comfortable silence to ask, "So, where are you taking me tonight?"

For the first time, Storm looked nervous. "About that…I thought about what you said this morning, about being tired and having to work double time to keep up with the mail, and I figured you might be okay with something low-key tonight."

"That sounds great," she said honestly.

"You have any issue with the media?" he asked. "I didn't see anyone outside your apartment."

"No issues. Media relations gave a briefing today and my name was mentioned as being the one who got the face full of tear gas. There were a few reporters hanging around when I got home, and I gave them a brief statement, and that was that. I think they're more interested in the rear admiral, since he was the target of the bomb. I feel bad for him, but I'm glad for me," Jane said with a smile.

"Dag will handle the press. Don't worry about him. I'm glad you won't be harassed."

"Me too," she told him."

It didn't dawn on her that Storm hadn't told her where they were going for dinner until they turned into a parking lot of a series of upscale townhouses not too far from the base. He pulled into a parking space, shut off his car, then turned to her. "I might be overstepping, but I thought I'd cook for you tonight. You can relax and not worry about anyone interrupting us while we eat."

"Does that happen a lot?" Jane asked curiously.

"What?"

"Being interrupted while you're on a date?"

"Well, I haven't been on a date in a very long time, but yeah, it's been known to happen a time or two. I just wanted you to be able to completely relax tonight. It's been a tough couple of days for you. But if it makes you uncomfortable, we can definitely go out somewhere."

Jane was shaking her head. "No, it's fine. But I have one question before I agree."

"Of course. You can ask me anything," Storm said.

"Can you cook?"

He grinned. "Yeah, Jane, I can cook."

"Good. Because I suck at it. I'd love to spend the evening with you at your place. But, I was serious earlier…I don't kiss on a first date."

"You're safe with me," Storm said seriously. "I'd never push you into doing anything you don't want to do."

"Thanks. I might be old, but I'm still safety conscious," she told him.

"You aren't old, and I have no problem with you wanting to be safe. Is there anyone you want to tell where you are tonight? Just in case?"

Jane appreciated him bringing it up. "I've already told my daughter that I'd be on a date tonight. She knows your name, rank, and where you work. I'll text her in a bit and give her your address. She might not care, but at least I've told someone, so if I end up chopped into tiny pieces and sprinkled around the city in various trash cans, someone will know who I was last with." She smiled, letting him know she was teasing…sort of.

Instead of being offended, Storm smiled even bigger. "Good. Come on, I've got some meal prep to do. I didn't want to start before I picked you up in case you wanted to go out somewhere instead."

Jane didn't give him a chance to come to her side of the car and open her door, but he was waiting for her when she got out, and he took her hand in his once more. It was crazy how quickly she was getting used to that. To him holding her hand as they walked. He kept half a step ahead of her, as if protecting her against anything that might come at them.

He led her to a unit on the end of the row and didn't drop her hand as he unlocked his door. He pushed it open and tugged her inside. He dropped his keys into a bowl sitting on a small table in the foyer and turned to her. "When you get tired, let me know, and I'll take you home."

"Thanks."

He looked at her for a moment, then said with a rueful smile, "The more time I spend with you, the more comfortable I am. It's kind of crazy."

"I feel the same," she reassured him.

He brought his hand up to her face and ran his thumb under her eye. "They're still a little red. Can you see all right? Nothing's blurry?"

Jane's heart melted at his concern. "I'm okay. The doc said the redness should go away in a day or so."

"I hate that it happened to you," Storm said softly. "I can't stand bullies. And the asshole who didn't have the balls to take his grievances to Dag directly is nothing but a bully."

For just a second, Jane saw the badass SEAL that Storm must've been. His eyes got hard, and if she'd been the target of his ire, she would've pissed her pants, but almost as soon as the fury and danger showed in his eyes, it disappeared. "Sorry, I didn't mean to bring it up."

"It's fine. And if I'm ever the target of something like that again, I'd want you on my side, that's for sure. You're kinda badass, Storm."

He smiled and shook his head. "Hopefully, you'll never see that part of me. I've done things I'm not exactly proud of in my lifetime. Killed a lot of people. I've done my best to put it behind me."

"I'm not sure it's healthy to forget what you've done. You have to learn to live with it and move on. For what it's worth, you're extremely respected…at least in my little corner of the world. You're never a dick to my employees and you never talk down to them even though they're just mail clerks. That means a lot. I mean, it has nothing to do with you killing people, people who I'm sure deserved to die because they were asshole terrorists, but the kind of person you are, a good one, shines through no matter what you've done in the past."

"Thank you," he told her. "And you and your employees aren't 'just' anything. You work hard and do your part to keep the base running smoothly."

"See? You're a nice guy."

"Except when someone I like and respect is threatened."

"Obviously," she told him with a smile. "Then I'd expect you to be a hardass and to kick some bad-guy butt."

Storm laughed, and Jane was glad to see some of the tension dissipate from his eyes.

"You said you couldn't cook, but how are you at chopping?"

"You mean other than that time I almost cut off the tip of my finger?" Jane asked. She couldn't help but laugh at the look of horror that entered his eyes. "Kidding! I'm kidding!" she reassured him. "I'm a pro at chopping."

"Maybe I'll let you tear the lettuce for the salad instead," Storm told her as he wrapped his arm around her waist and gave her a small hug before tugging her toward his kitchen.

As she chuckled, Jane realized that she hadn't laughed as much in the last year as she had in the last day and a half. Even with being sprayed with tear gas, she'd been happier than she'd been in a very long time.

Simply being around Storm made her smile.

Please don't be playing me, she pleaded silently as Storm got her situated on a barstool and headed for the refrigerator to get her a head of lettuce to prepare their salad.

* * * *

Storm looked down at the woman sleeping against his side, and smiled.

He'd had more fun tonight than he'd had in a very long time. She'd prepared the salad while he'd prepped the steaks he'd bought on his way home before picking her up. While they were cooking, they'd talked about everything from where they'd grown up to their loathing of the traffic in the Southern California area.

Conversation flowed easily, and not once did things feel awkward. She didn't hesitate to help with the dishes and laughed when she'd seen his collection of funny mugs he'd acquired over the years.

After dinner had been cleared away, they'd settled on his couch to watch—what else—*Shawshank Redemption*, and she'd fallen asleep within minutes. Storm knew he should wake her up and take her home, but he was enjoying holding her as she slept. She'd put her head on his shoulder when they'd sat down and hadn't protested when he'd wrapped an arm around her.

Storm had no idea what it was about Jane that felt so right. He'd been on a lot of first dates, and none had been as satisfying as this one. Maybe it was because the pressure of sex was off the table. She'd made her stance more than clear on that, and honestly, it was a relief. Storm craved a deeper connection with someone, and with Jane, he was getting just that.

On the television screen, the part in *Shawshank* where Andy Dufresne put on the Italian opera started, and the music was loud in the room around them. Jane stirred and opened her eyes.

"Crap, I fell asleep," she muttered.

Storm couldn't help but smile again. "You did," he agreed.

"It's rude. You should've nudged me."

"No way in hell was that gonna happen. You've had a hard couple of days. Besides, it's not a hardship holding you," Storm told her.

He loved how she blushed.

"You want me to take you home?" he asked.

He was thrilled when she shook her head. "Not yet…if that's okay. I'm really comfortable. And we haven't gotten to the good part in the movie yet. I love the ending when Red narrates and wraps everything up."

"It's more than okay," Storm reassured her.

"Can you tell me about your teams?" she asked.

"Wow, that was out of the blue," he teased.

Jane chuckled. "Yeah, my mind works in weird ways. Earlier, you said something about your men managing to have loving relationships while being on a SEAL team. That got me to thinking about what happened recently in the parking lot of our building, with that crazy woman trying to shoot that SEAL, and how his girlfriend crawled under the cars to grab her ankles. And that got me thinking about how hard it must've been for you to have to punish Phantom for disobeying your order and going overseas to rescue his girlfriend, even though they weren't dating at the time. And *that* got me thinking about how difficult it must be to balance being their boss and their friend."

Storm chuckled. He loved getting an insight to the way her mind worked. He scooted down a bit on the couch and sighed in contentment when Jane snuggled deeper into him. "I'm not sure where to start," he admitted.

"How many teams are you working with?"

"Three. And that might not sound like a lot, but it's important to me to investigate everything about where they might be sent so they aren't heading into a situation with incomplete information. It's a lot of work. And when one team is deployed on a mission, I'm still researching other areas of the world where the other two might be sent. Not to mention assisting their families with anything that might come up, as well as the government red tape. It keeps me busy."

Jane snorted. "Understatement of the year," she said under her breath. "Tell me about the team who was involved in the parking lot incident."

"You already know Phantom was the one who was targeted. A woman he dated became obsessed with him and decided if she couldn't have him, no one could. As you know, it was handled quickly, and luckily without anyone getting hurt."

"I heard you basically gave him a slap on the wrist for disobeying your orders...was that a hard decision?"

"Not at all," Storm told her. "What he did was stupid, simply because he could've gotten hurt. He went in to get Kalee without any backup, which could've ended very badly. But here's the thing...it's exactly the kind of action I would've taken when I was his age. The thought of that young woman being stranded overseas was horrifying, but without the approval of the Timor-Leste government to go back in, our hands were tied."

"She's okay though?" Jane asked.

Storm nodded. "She is. She's amazing. And I'm proud as hell of Phantom. I'm glad things are working out between him and Kalee. He deserves to have someone as strong as she is by his side. They all do. Rocco, Gumby, Ace, Bubba, and Rex...they're good men who do whatever is asked of them without complaint. I'm glad they each have someone to come home to."

"Was anyone there for you when you came home from missions?" she asked.

Storm sighed. "Not really. There were women here and there, but none could handle the secrecy that came along with my job. They didn't like not knowing where I was or when I would be home. And they *really* didn't like that I couldn't tell them anything about the missions when I returned. Some assumed I was cheating on them because of all the secrecy, and others just got fed up with me not being around."

"That wasn't fair," Jane said softly.

"It was what it was," Storm said matter-of-factly. "Honestly, most of the time it was a relief when they called it off. I can't say I was the best boyfriend, and like I mentioned, I didn't think it was fair to put someone through the heartache and worry that comes with being the partner of a SEAL. I'm proud as hell of my men. It's not easy to be a SEAL and have a family."

Storm looked down to find Jane studying him intently. "What?" he asked.

"I just...you sound like you're resigned to being single."

Storm thought about that for a second. "I guess I kinda am. I mean, I'm not on a SEAL team anymore, but I'm just as busy now as I was when I was younger. I might not be on the front line fighting, but I'm just as invested as I was then. I work long hours, and I'm not sure anyone would want to put up with that."

He wanted to take the words back as soon as he said them, but they were already out there.

"When my husband left me, I was so busy trying to keep my head above water and a roof over our heads that I didn't have time to think about dating again. Then, when Rose was going through her issues, I couldn't think about anyone but her. I worried about her for quite a few years after she moved out, because I knew she was out there doing drugs and other dangerous things. It's only been in the last five years or so that I've even thought about wanting to share my life with a man again.

"But…it's not as easy to find someone who's serious about wanting a relationship at my age as it was when I was in my twenties. The guys I've dated have either seemed to want a sugar mama to pay for everything so they can stay home and watch sports all day, or they're turned off that I don't *need* them. I've gotten used to my own company, and I make enough money now to be comfortable. That scares a lot of men."

"It doesn't scare me," Storm assured her. "Actually, it's a relief. I mean, I'm happy you make your own money and can obviously take care of yourself."

They smiled at each other for a beat.

"I'm just sorry it took me so long to notice you," Storm said honestly.

Jane shrugged. "Maybe it just wasn't the right time."

"Maybe not," Storm agreed. "Although I'm glad I got my head out of my ass the other morning. When I heard you were in trouble, I couldn't think about anything other than getting to you."

"I'm still embarrassed about that," Jane admitted.

"Why?"

"Why? Because you found me on my hands and knees, snot running out of my nose and having just puked my guts out. Then I had to get naked in front of you. Not exactly the way I imagined you finally *noticing* me."

"You want to know what I saw when I entered the mail room?" Storm asked.

"No," Jane said, but nodded her head as she did.

Storm grinned, then got serious. "I saw a woman who'd selflessly sent all of her employees out of harm's way. Who was bent, but not broken. And trust me, the first time I inhaled CS gas, I reacted much worse than you…and I didn't get a direct hit to my face."

She raised an eyebrow in disbelief.

"I did," he insisted. "I pissed my pants while it felt as if I was coughing up a lung."

Storm loved the smile Jane tried to hide from him. "Seriously?"

"Yup." Then he brought a hand to her face and tilted her chin up so she had to look at him. "Don't be embarrassed. First, because you were reacting in a completely normal way. I'll invite you out to watch the guys in boot camp as they go through the CS gas training so you can see for yourself. And secondly, while it wasn't exactly appropriate for the time and place, you have absolutely nothing to be worried about when it comes to your body."

She snorted in disbelief.

"I'm serious. You've got curves in all the right places, Jane…and there's nothing I like more than a woman's softness against my hardness." Storm knew his words were a bit crude, and could have more than one meaning, but he was being completely honest. He'd had enough of women with so-called "perfect" bodies. He wanted a *real* woman. Someone who wasn't afraid to eat and whose skin he could sink his fingers into. Jane definitely fit that bill.

"My ex used to call me Plain Jane," she admitted.

Storm caressed her face gently. "He was an idiot, I think that's more than obvious with the way he cheated on you and left you and your daughter to fend for yourselves."

He stayed still as Jane's gaze bored into his own. He had no idea what she was thinking but hoped he hadn't been too honest. Too open.

When she sighed and turned her head back toward the TV and settled against him once more, Storm let out a breath of relief.

"This is crazy," she muttered. "I've crushed on you so hard for so long…I have no idea how this is even happening."

Storm smiled. "I got my head out of my ass," he reminded her.

She chuckled, and Storm relaxed even further.

They both turned their attention back to the movie and watched Jane's favorite part…Red narrating how Andy escaped from the prison. It wasn't until Red was walking down the beach in Mexico toward his old friend that Jane looked up at Storm once more. "This movie never gets old."

"Nope," Storm agreed.

As the credits rolled, Jane yawned hugely.

"Time to get you home," Storm told her. He hated to see her leave, but they both had work in the morning, and he knew she was exhausted.

"Thank you for dinner," she told him as they stood.

"You're more than welcome."

"I'd say next time it's on me, but you already know that I can't cook."

Storm loved what she was saying without words and couldn't help teasing her a little. "You askin' me out for a second date?"

"If I was, would you say yes?"

"Abso-fucking-lutely."

"Then I guess I am."

"Good. I'm looking forward to it."

"Me too," Jane said shyly.

"Come on, Cinderella, let's get you back to your apartment before you turn into a pumpkin."

"I think you've got your fairy tales mixed up," she said with a chuckle.

Storm didn't give a shit about fairy tales, so he simply smiled.

He held her hand all the way home as he drove, and this time when he pulled up to the curb, he climbed out of the car and walked her to the door of the apartment complex. He took her hand once more and brought it up to his mouth and kissed the back. "Thanks for coming over," he told her.

"Thanks for asking me."

"Sleep well."

"I have a feeling I will," she said with a small smile.

"I'll see you in the morning?" he asked.

Jane nodded. "Probably. We're supposed to be able to get back into the mail room, so things will be crazy busy until we get back into the swing of things and clear out the backlog of packages and mail."

"Don't work too hard," Storm told her.

"I could say the same to you," she quipped.

Storm squeezed her hand then dropped it and took a step back. He wanted to kiss her. Badly. But he respected her no-kissing-on-the-first-date thing. "I'll be in touch," he told her.

Jane nodded.

"Go inside, sweetheart," he ordered.

With one last long look at him, she turned and entered the lobby of her apartment complex, giving him a small, adorable wave before heading for the elevators. Storm went back to his car and climbed inside. All the way home, he thought about the last few hours. About how much he'd enjoyed hanging out with Jane. She was…comforting. He didn't feel the need to constantly entertain her or to keep the conversation going. Whenever there were lulls, they felt natural. Right.

Pretty much everything about her felt right. It should've scared the shit out of him, but instead it just made him more determined to get to know her better. He knew it had been years since her ex had left her, but he still thought the man was an idiot. Though that idiocy had opened the door for Storm today, so he couldn't be too upset.

How he'd gone from confirmed bachelor to being infatuated with a woman in a day and a half, Storm had no idea, but he wasn't going to question it. Too many things had happened in his life that could be called miracles for him to wonder about the timing of finally seeing what was right in front of him.

For the first time in a very long time, Storm was excited about something other than work. He had no idea what the future would hold for him and Jane, but he was going to work damn hard to be the kind of man she deserved.

Chapter Five

Jane looked down at her phone and smiled at the text she'd just received from Storm. It had been two weeks since their first date, and they'd only managed to get together one other time since then, but they'd talked via text and phone every day.

Storm: I've got twenty minutes before I have to head into my next meeting...any chance you can find some mail of mine and bring it up to my office? :)

Things had been hectic for them both, her because of the increased safety measures of examining every piece of incoming mail and still getting caught up from the bombing incident, and Storm because one of his teams was on a mission and he'd been working overtime to make sure they were safe and had every piece of available information while they were gone.

They'd both been free one day around lunch and had gone to the base cafeteria together for their second date. It hadn't been as satisfying as being able to completely relax as they'd done in his townhouse, but she still loved seeing Storm in business mode. Seeing him in his blue BDUs did something for her. He was handsome and demanded respect from everyone around him. About ten years ago, she probably would've been ashamed to be seen with him—after all, she was merely a contract worker—but now she was older and wiser, and Jane was proud to be with him.

She grabbed a stack of letters and inter-base envelopes addressed to him and told her employees that she'd be gone a while. Everyone in the mail room seemed to have gotten closer after the bomb incident. They all knew it could've been any of them who'd gotten the tear gas in their faces, and they all seemed to be looking out for each other a little closer as the days went by.

NCIS had been in to interview everyone in the mail room, but Jane hadn't heard anything about them being any closer to finding the person who'd sent the bomb.

Putting thoughts of that out of her head, she climbed the stairs to the top floor where Storm's office was located.

She greeted the few people she passed with a friendly smile and felt butterflies in her belly at the thought of seeing Storm again. It was silly, but she couldn't help it. He'd exceeded her expectations and daydreams tenfold. She never thought he'd be as attentive as he was...even when they didn't see each other.

But letting her know that he wouldn't mind seeing her when he had a quick break meant the world to her. Her ex always made her feel as if she was being silly when she'd lamented the fact she didn't get to see him much, so Storm inviting her up when he had twenty minutes to spare made her very happy.

She entered his outer office and smiled at his administrative assistant. "Hi," she said cheerily.

"Hey, Jane. Thank God you're here. He's been in a hell of a mood. I know seeing you will make him a bit less of a grump."

Jane laughed. "I'll do my best, but no promises." She was relieved his right-hand man didn't seem to have any issues with them seeing each other. Apparently, Storm had come right out and admitted to his admin that they were dating, and that she was welcome in his office any time he wasn't in a meeting.

It felt good not to be a naughty little secret.

Jane walked over to Storm's office door and knocked softly. She pushed it open a crack and said, "Storm?"

"Come in," he called out.

Jane entered the room, shutting the door behind her. "Hey," she said almost shyly when she was in front of his desk.

"Come here," Storm said, holding out an arm.

Jane walked around his desk to his side, not knowing exactly what to expect, and put the mail she'd brought for him on his desk.

When she was by his side, Storm reached up and put a hand behind her neck. He gently urged her to bend, and when she did, he kissed her lightly on the lips.

It was just a peck, but the jolt that went through her body was immediate and made goose bumps break out on her arms. It was their first kiss, and while it wasn't exactly intimate, it was still shocking in its intensity.

"Shit, sorry," Storm said, letting go of her neck and rubbing a hand over his face. "I didn't mean to overstep."

"It's…it's fine," Jane reassured him. She took a longer look at him and realized that he looked very stressed out. He was frowning and had deep lines on his forehead. Without thought, she pushed some papers out of her way and sat on his desk next to him. "Are you all right?" she asked quietly.

Storm sighed. "I'm tired," he admitted.

"Your team?" she asked.

"They're okay. They ran into some problems, but they're all alive and relatively unscathed. They'll be home within twenty-four hours. Thank God."

"Good," Jane said. She reached out and took one of his hands in hers. She rested his palm on her thigh and ran her thumb over the back of his hand.

"Damn, it's good to see you," Storm said, scooting his chair to the side, then forward, resting his free arm on his desk next to her hip.

Jane could feel the heat from his body against her own, and while she was sitting higher than he was, looking down at him, she still felt surrounded by him. "When your team gets home…will you have time to come over for dinner?" she asked. "I mean, I suck at cooking, but that doesn't mean that I can't order a kick-ass dinner from one of my favorite restaurants."

He looked up at her. "I'd like that a lot," he said.

"Good."

"I'm sorry I haven't been around much," he told her.

Jane shook her head. "Don't. I knew what I was getting into when I agreed to go out with you. Hell, you all but spelled it out when I was at your house. I like who you are, Storm. I like that you're worried about your men. I admire you. The fact that you've been taking the time out of your very busy schedule to text me, to call, to let me know you're thinking about me even if you don't have time to see me, means everything."

"You deserve better," he said softly.

"Than what? A man who texts me just to let me know he misses me? Someone who leaves me a long voice message because he randomly thought about the part in our favorite movie where Andy tells Red that hope is a good thing, the best of things, and no good thing ever dies...and that he hopes our relationship works out because he can't stop thinking about me? Lord, Storm, you've been more attentive to me in the last two weeks, without seeing me, than any other man has been *in person.* You have nothing to apologize for."

Storm squeezed the hand that was lying on her thigh and curled the other around her ass. Then he surprised her by leaning over and resting his forehead against her knee. Jane brought a hand up to run her fingers through his hair.

How long they sat like that she wasn't sure, but she felt more connected to Storm than she'd ever felt with another man. Ever. It should've scared her. Hell, they hadn't even really kissed or spent much time together, but he'd shown by his actions that he wasn't like the boys she'd dated in the past. He was a grown-ass man, an honorable one. One she was desperate to get to know intimately.

They both heard Storm's administrative assistant greeting someone out in the other room at the same time. Storm's head came up, and he squeezed her hand one last time. Jane saw the mask fall over his features. Right in front of her eyes, he changed from the tired man to the ever-so-competent and in-control admiral.

When someone knocked on the door, Jane stood up and faced the door.

"Come in," Storm called.

Rear Admiral Dag Creasy appeared in the doorway.

"Dag," Storm said with a smile. "Good to see you."

"Same," the other man said, returning his smile.

Jane started to slide sideways to get out of their hair, but the rear admiral gestured for her to stay. "Don't go, Jane. I didn't mean to interrupt."

"But you did," Storm told his friend in mock irritation. "So get on with it so I can get back to some quiet time with my girl before the shit hits the fan again."

Dag didn't take offense. He merely smiled and sat in one of the chairs in front of Storm's desk.

Jane wasn't sure what to do. Should she stay where she was? Go sit in the other chair? Leave? She'd always liked the rear admiral, but she didn't really know him and wasn't sure what the protocol was in an instance like this.

"Heard anything from NCIS about the person who mailed that bomb to you?" Storm asked as he reached out and pulled Jane closer to him. She stumbled slightly, but ended up resting on the arm of his chair. Storm's arm went around her waist to steady her, and she barely breathed as she sat perched next to him.

"That's why I'm here," Dag said, leaning back, not seeming at all surprised or irritated that she was practically sitting in Storm's lap. "I was sent the preliminary report today, and I wanted to talk to you about it."

"I should go," Jane said again.

"Stay," Dag ordered. "This concerns you as much as anyone else. After all, you were the one who bore the brunt of the asshole's anger. It's only fair."

"What'd they find out?" Storm asked.

Jane had to admit she was curious, so she stayed where she was and listened with rapt attention.

"There was a note inside the box that was recovered and pieced back together. The person who wrote it obviously isn't happy with me. They rambled on and on about what a shit officer I am and how I'm unfit to be in charge of anyone. The person said that I held grudges and punished sailors unfairly. NCIS believes it was sent by someone who was court-martialed while under my command."

"That should narrow things down considerably," Storm said. "That's good, isn't it?"

Dag shrugged. "Yes and no. I mean, it makes sense that it's someone who was court-martialed recently, but what if it's not? There have been hundreds of sailors who have been disciplined over the years under my command."

"What about the handwriting on the box? Can they somehow track that?" Jane asked, then blushed as both men looked at her. "Uh…sorry, I'm sure they've thought of that."

"They have," Dag said with a small smile. "And it's a no-go. The Navy doesn't keep handwriting samples of their sailors. As you know, there was no return address and the stamps were hand-canceled, so that makes it harder to track. The ink was smudged and it's unreadable, so there's no way of knowing how the box got into the mail system in the first place."

Jane nodded. "Yeah, that does make it tougher. It could've been dropped off by hand or sent through the mail system off the base. Are you still in danger, Sir?"

Dag's expression gentled. "I can take care of myself," he said.

Which wasn't an answer. "Of course you can," Jane agreed. "But forgive me for overstepping here—what if the person decides to step things up? Putting tear gas in a box is one thing, but they might decide to hand-deliver a box to your beautiful home on the ocean. It could be an actual bomb next time. What else is NCIS doing to find out who did this so you can be safe? The last thing you need to worry about when you leave work is someone coming after you, especially after all you've done for your country."

Her voice had risen by the time she was done, and Jane realized that she was practically shouting and blushed.

"I like her," Dag said, looking at Storm.

"She's likable," Storm agreed. "And you've got your own, so eyes off."

Jane looked between the two men, torn between embarrassment and disbelief at their banter.

"To answer your question, Jane," Dag said, acting as if the exchange between him and Storm hadn't happened, "NCIS is doing all they can to figure this out. The last thing I want is another innocent getting caught between whoever this is and myself. It's dishonorable of him to put anyone else in danger because of his own grievances. If I get a package delivered to my house that I'm not expecting, you can bet I'd never pick it up without making damn sure it was safe. I haven't had a chance to tell you personally yet, but I'm very sorry you got caught in the middle of this…whatever it is."

"It's not your fault, Sir," she told him.

"Maybe, maybe not. That remains to be seen. But please stay extra vigilant. Until we find out how that package got through our mail system, no one is safe. Like you said, the last thing I want is to worry about someone else getting hurt," the rear admiral said.

"I will. We will. We're being very careful," Jane told him.

"I saw your interview on the news," Dag said. "Has the press backed off you yet?"

Jane nodded. "Yeah, they've been pretty good, actually. They wanted to know the details about what happened to me, but once they realized I was just a random victim, they lost interest pretty fast."

"Just be careful, because whoever sent that package could've seen the coverage and might turn their ire on *you*."

"Me?" Jane asked in surprise.

"Yeah. They didn't succeed in getting to *me*, the person they were aiming for, and in their mind, they might think you prevented it."

"That's crazy," Jane said.

"Sending a mail bomb *is* crazy," Dag said with a shrug. "You should be extra careful until whoever sent the package has been caught."

It had been a long time since someone had worried about her. And now in the span of two weeks, two larger-than-life men were trying to look out for her. She knew Dag was happily married, but it still felt good. Really good.

"He's right," Storm said. "I hadn't really thought about that, but Dag's exactly right."

"Nothing's happened," Jane tried to reassure both of them. "I'm fine."

"I'll keep a closer eye on her," Storm told Dag.

Jane wanted to be upset that he was talking around her, but she couldn't bring herself to be. Not when it was obvious he was concerned.

"You need help going through the records of the recent court-martials?" Storm asked the rear admiral.

Jane winced, as she knew Storm's plate was already more than full, but she wasn't really surprised he'd offered.

"Thank you, but no. I know you have no extra time to look for a needle in a haystack. But I'll keep you in the loop because I have a feeling this isn't over. Whoever sent that CS gas bomb wanted me to suffer, and because I didn't, no doubt they aren't happy. It could be tomorrow or three months from now. There's no telling when whoever this is will try again."

Jane shivered, and Storm must've felt it because he squeezed her hips reassuringly.

Then the rear admiral changed the subject. "Your team's getting home soon, right?"

"Yeah, tomorrow night if everything goes well," Storm told him.

"I expect you to take at least forty-eight hours off," Dag said sternly.

Storm opened his mouth to protest, but the rear admiral cut him off. "No buts. I know you've got other teams and things to do, but you've been burning the candle at both ends lately. Take the time off. Sleep. Relax. Read a damn book. I don't care what you do, but I don't want to hear you've been at the office. Understand?"

"Yes, Sir," Storm said.

Dag chuckled. "Most people would be pleased to get time off."

"I am," Storm insisted. "There's nothing I'd like better than to spend time with Jane."

"Good," Dag said. "I just wish it was under better circumstances."

"As far as I'm concerned, there's nothing I want to do more than hang out with Jane and make sure whoever is behind this bomb doesn't get a second chance to cause havoc."

His words made Jane feel good. She didn't like keeping him from work, but she loved that he wasn't upset about taking work off to spend with her.

"It's not easy dating a sailor," Dag said, looking at Jane again, "but I can guarantee that even when Storm's not with you, he's probably thinking about you. I know that's how I feel about my Brenae. I'll leave you two then."

"You'll let me know if you get any leads on the bomber?" Storm asked, standing up and reaching out to shake Dag's hand as Jane stood as well.

"Of course," the rear admiral said. Then he nodded at Storm and Jane and turned and left the office, closing the door behind him as he went.

Storm being Storm, he didn't hesitate to act. He turned to her and wrapped one arm around her waist, and the other snuck into the hair at her nape. He pulled her into him, and Jane could feel every inch of his hard body against hers. She flushed, wondering if this was even allowed...an officer consorting with a contractor in his office.

But the door was shut, and it was just the two of them.

"Tomorrow night is Friday," he said quietly.

"I know," Jane said with a small frown.

"Apparently I've got the weekend off. After my men arrive home and we finish the debrief, I'm free for forty-eight hours."

"Good. You need the break," she said.

"I'd like to spend that time with *you*," Storm said. "As much of it as you'll give me."

Jane wasn't sure what he was asking, but she was more than willing to agree. "Okay."

"Just like that?" he asked.

Jane nodded. "Yeah. I'm not into games. I like you, Storm. I want to spend time with you. Get to know you better. I know it's not usual for you to have so much time off, so I'm okay with being greedy and wanting to hoard it all for myself."

He grinned. "Good. We've had two dates," he reminded her.

"You're counting that lunch the other day as a date too?" she asked with a smile.

"Absolutely. And you told me before we had dinner you don't kiss on the first date, but what about the third?"

Jane couldn't help but smile. "I might...with the right man."

He smiled back then said, "I didn't mean to jump the gun earlier. It was instinctive. I saw you, and you were such a bright light in my exhaustion that I acted without thinking and kissed you."

"You think that was a kiss?" Jane sassed.

His smile grew.

"I'll have you know, Storm North, that a small peck on the lips isn't a real kiss in my book. I'm gonna want a true kiss on our third date," she told him, feeling braver than she'd ever felt before. She'd wanted this man forever, and she'd be damned if she acted like a shy ninny and let her heart's desire slip through her fingers. She'd learned over the years that if she wanted something, she had to work her ass off for it.

"Noted," he said with such a look of desire on his face, it made her want to attack him right then and there. "So you won't mind if I give you another *peck*, as you called it, before you leave to go back to work? Since that doesn't count?"

"No," Jane told him, holding her breath in anticipation.

He leaned toward her ever so slowly, his gaze not leaving hers. Jane couldn't keep her eyes open, closing them seconds before his lips touched her forehead. Then he kissed her nose. Then her cheeks...

By the time he moved to her lips, she was ready to jump out of her skin. Jane could feel her nipples harden under the sensible work polo she wore every day and dampness between her thighs. She wanted Storm with every fiber of her being. And it had been a very long time since she'd felt true desire for a man. She'd been too busy, and besides, her vibrator took care of her urges when she had them.

But she had a feeling nothing could douse the lust coursing through her body except for the man holding her right that moment.

His lips finally brushed against her own, and she couldn't stop the small whimper that escaped. She felt him smile against her lips as he kissed her again. Small little pecks that did nothing to assuage her need. All it did was stoke the flames higher.

When his lips brushed hers again, she licked them and felt his moan throughout her body. Smiling, she opened her eyes and stared into his own.

"For the first time in a very long time, I'm looking forward to my days off," Storm told her quietly.

"Me too," Jane echoed.

They heard the admin greeting someone else in the outer office, and Storm groaned. "That's my next appointment."

Jane nodded. She tried to step back, but Storm's hands on her body didn't let go. He held her to him for a brief moment, and she was happy to see the same disappointment she felt echoed in his gaze.

"I'm not sure how this happened, but I'm damn glad it did," he said then leaned forward, kissed her hard on the lips, and dropped his arms before taking a step back.

"Me too," Jane told him.

"I hope you really heard what Dag said," Storm reminded her seriously. "Don't take your safety for granted. Here at work or at home. All right?"

"I won't," Jane told him. She was always safety conscious. Being a single woman with a daughter had forced her to see boogeymen behind every corner and to be hyper-aware of her surroundings. As a man, a muscular, badass man, Storm probably had no idea the kinds of situations someone like her had to worry about on a daily basis. But now wasn't the time to get into that. "Let me know when you get home?" she asked.

"I will. You do the same. I want to know that you're safe and sound behind your door."

Jane nodded. She liked that he worried about her.

"I'm glad your men are coming home," she told him.

"Me too. I'll talk to you later, and we can make plans for the weekend," he said.

"Okay." She backed up and turned at the last second to open the door.

"Thanks for bringing up my mail," Storm said loud enough for the lieutenant who was waiting in the outer office to hear.

"You're welcome," she responded, knowing he was doing what he could to protect her reputation, not his own. She nodded at Storm's admin, who winked at her, then she headed out into the hall and toward the stairs.

Bringing a hand to her lips, she touched them and smiled. Yeah, she could safely say she was looking forward to the weekend more than she had in a very long time.

Chapter Six

Storm parked his car and eagerly climbed out and headed for the lobby of Jane's apartment. He'd been glad to see for himself that all of the SEALs on his team were alive and well when they'd arrived back into the country. He'd just spent two hours in a debrief meeting with them and was now clear to enjoy his forty-eight hours of leave.

He'd offered to cook for Jane, but she'd declined, saying there was no way she was going to make him cook after working late into the evening.

It was now seven-thirty, and he'd been at the office for over twelve hours. Storm was more than ready for a break. He walked down the hall to Jane's apartment and knocked on the door. It took a few seconds, but then she was there, smiling and welcoming him into her home.

"You look tired," she blurted, then wrinkled her nose. "Sorry, that was rude. Come in."

Storm didn't take offense. "I *am* tired," he told her.

"Your guys are all right, though?"

He liked that she asked about them. "They are. The mission was tough, but they're all back relatively unharmed."

"Ugh, I hate that," she said, more to herself than him. "I mean, I'm glad they're home, but 'relatively unharmed' can have so much hidden meaning to it. It could mean they've all got bullet holes in them, but are still walking and talking, or it could mean they've got a few little bruises."

Storm chuckled, and when she turned to face him after closing and locking her front door, he pulled her into him. She let out a small *oof* of surprise but recovered quickly. Her hands rested on his chest, and he could smell that she'd showered recently.

"Storm?" she asked.

"Sorry," he told her. "The guys are all right. One got shot, but it was only a graze. The mission went a little sideways, but they got done what needed to be done." Storm knew he was being vague, but he couldn't talk about where his team had been or what they'd been doing. He tensed, waiting for her reaction, remembering too many other conversations like this with women that had *also* gone sideways.

"Well, good," she said with a small nod. "I ordered from Leroy's Kitchen and Lounge. They know me very well there, since I love me some fancy food. I got you the house-made bucatini...pork sausage, mushrooms, basil, pesto, and ricotta salad. I got myself the whole-fried branzino, which has basmati rice, red African curry, chili oil, and cilantro. It's very spicy, but I love it. If you don't want the bucatini, though, I'm happy to switch with you...or we can just order a pizza. I've got our meals warming in the oven because I wasn't sure exactly when you were going to get here... Why are you looking at me like that?"

Storm didn't have to ask her what she meant. He knew he was staring at her as if she had two heads. "You aren't going to ask me for more details about the guys' mission?"

She frowned as if confused. "No. I know you can't tell me. I appreciate you saying as much as you did. Why...should I?"

"No," he said quickly. "I just...most people aren't as...accepting as you are when I can't tell them details about my work."

"Storm," Jane said gently. "I get it. I might be only a mail chick, but I do understand confidentiality and top-secret clearances."

"Don't do that," he scolded.

"Do what?" she asked with a small tilt of her head, genuinely oblivious.

"Don't belittle yourself. You aren't 'only' a mail chick. You've worked hard to get to where you are. Own it. Be proud of it. You run a tight ship, and I, for one, am very thankful I don't have to track down correspondence that I know I should've received, and I never worry about my reports and other documents getting to where they need to go safely and securely."

"You're right," Jane said a little sheepishly. "I just...you're larger than life to me, and I still have to pinch myself that you're here. Sometimes my insecurities get the best of me."

"Well, you have nothing to worry about. And...bucatini? You really got me bucatini?"

She smiled. "I did."

"Damn," he said on a sigh. "I could get used to you 'cooking' for me. But honestly, it's too much. Leroy's Kitchen isn't cheap."

"Can I tell you a secret?" she asked.

"Of course," he told her immediately.

"Leroy feels sorry for me and gives me a kick-ass discount," she told him with a grin. "I think I've put at least two of his kids through college with how much I eat there, so it's only fair."

Storm laughed and felt his muscles relaxing for the first time that day. "Red, I do believe you're talking out of your ass," he replied, quoting *Shawshank*.

Jane looked confused for a millisecond, then she threw her head back and laughed. "I'm not, I swear I'm not. And...good usage of the movie quote."

Storm felt ten years younger just standing in her foyer bantering with her. Just the thought of how she could've been badly hurt if the bomb that had exploded in her hands had been anything other than tear gas physically hurt his heart.

And remembering how he'd decided he was going to take things slow, get to know her at work before attempting to ask her out, made him shake his head in disbelief. If he'd done that, he would've missed out on this right here. And missing out on one second of time with Jane Hamilton suddenly seemed like the stupidest decision ever.

"I needed this," he said softly.

"What?" she asked.

"This. You. Preparing dinner, even if that preparation was ordering it from one of your favorite restaurants. Quoting *Shawshank* and having you know what the hell I'm talking about. Forgetting about work for a few hours and simply relaxing with a funny, beautiful, and charming woman who doesn't get pissed when I can't talk about my job."

Her face gentled, and Storm could see how much his words meant to her. "Me too," she said. "I mean, I didn't have to deal with the aftermath of a mission like you did today, but NCIS came down to talk to me again after I was in your office—and they scared the shit out of me, giving me all sorts of dire warnings about how the bomber might come after me, that the news made it seem like I'd foiled his great plan of getting to the rear admiral. Basically saying the same thing as Dag."

"Come 'ere," Storm said, pulling her even closer into him, resting his hand on the back of her head as she rested her cheek against his chest.

They stood in each other's embrace in her hallway for a long moment, taking solace and comfort from one another.

"I'm sorry," he said after a while.

"Not your fault," Jane returned immediately. "And it's not that I don't believe the investigators, it just doesn't make sense that someone would get upset with *me*. I was just in the wrong place at the wrong time, collateral damage."

Storm pulled back and put his hands on her face. He was only a few inches taller than her, and so they were almost eye to eye. "Even so…be careful, okay?"

"Of course."

"I'll tell you if I find out anything else about who he might be."

"Can you do that?" she asked.

"Yes," Storm said, even though he wasn't one hundred percent sure of his answer. If the person behind the mail bomb was a former SEAL, or one of Creasy's sailors, he might not be at liberty to give her any details, but he could give her as much information as possible to keep her safe and still retain confidentiality.

For the first time in his career, Storm knew he would breach security and tell her what she needed to know to keep herself safe…even if that meant he would get in trouble.

And just like that, Storm had a better understanding of what Phantom had felt when he'd disobeyed a direct order to head overseas and rescue Kalee Solberg.

"Come on," Jane said softly. "You need food."

Storm smiled when his stomach chose that moment to growl.

"See?" she said with a smile. Then she grabbed hold of his hand still on her face and tugged him deeper into her apartment.

He couldn't help but let his gaze drop to her ass as she led him to the small table next to her kitchen. Jane had what some people might call a bubble butt. It seemed like such a derogatory term when others said it, but as he stared at her gorgeous body, he couldn't agree. His hands itched to get ahold of her. To watch the fleshy globes shimmy and shake as he took her from behind. It was a visceral image, and Storm felt like an ass for even thinking it.

He and Jane weren't that far in their relationship. Hell, they hadn't even kissed yet. *Really* kissed. He shouldn't be thinking about fucking her...and yet he couldn't stop his mind from fantasizing about how beautiful she'd be lying under him, her brown hair fanned out on his pillow, her back arched with her luscious tits thrust up for his mouth. How she'd spread her legs for him, and how amazing her heat would feel around his cock.

"Storm?" she asked, and he forced his mind out of the gutter. Jane deserved more from him than base urges. He needed to be better.

"Yeah?"

"You looked like you were a million miles away," she said.

"You're beautiful," he blurted, and watched as she blushed. "I mean it."

Jane shrugged. "I'm just me," she told him. Something she'd said before.

"Yes, you are," he agreed. Then, knowing he wouldn't be able to sit across from her throughout dinner without thinking about touching her, kissing her, Storm tugged her toward him.

And once more she stumbled into him, her hands landing on his chest.

"This is our third date," he reminded her.

And thank fuck she knew exactly what he was getting at.

"Looks like the world—and you—went and got itself in a big damn hurry," she quipped.

Her quote from Brooks in *Shawshank* made him even harder. He raised an eyebrow, asking permission to kiss her.

In response, Jane went up on her tiptoes and put her hand on the back of his neck. She pulled him toward her, and the second their lips touched, Storm knew he was a goner.

He'd tried to tell himself that he should take things slow, but he'd been living in a fantasy world.

It seemed as if he'd been kissing this woman forever, but at the same time, he knew he'd never felt anything like this before in his life. Jane might do her best to fade into the background at work, but there was nothing timid about her actions at the moment. Her fingernails dug into the flesh at the back of his neck and made him shiver as he pulled her even closer.

Storm tilted his head in order to take her deeper, and at the same time he eased his tongue inside her mouth. She moaned, opening wider to let him in. He couldn't help but imitate what he'd been fantasizing about earlier, kissing her harder, plunging his tongue in and out of her mouth in a crude facsimile of sex.

And Jane took everything he gave her. She sucked on his tongue and groaned when he nipped her lower lip before sinking inside her mouth once more.

How long they stood by her table making out Storm had no idea, but it wasn't until he felt a little light-headed from lack of oxygen that he pulled back a fraction.

Jane immediately lowered her head. He felt her inhale deeply as if trying to take his essence inside her body...then her hot tongue licked the tendon at the side of his neck. Storm's cock was rock hard and digging into her belly, but Jane didn't flinch away from him. No, there was nothing shy about Jane at that point of time, and Storm fucking loved it.

Just when he felt her hands brushing down the sides of the polo shirt he'd changed into before heading to her house, his stomach once more made its emptiness known by growling long and loud.

Amazingly, Jane giggled against him, and Storm could feel every puff of air against the sensitive skin of his neck...which did nothing to cool his ardor.

"I need to feed you," Jane said as she lifted her head.

Storm inhaled deeply through his nose when he got a look at her face. Her lips were pink and swollen, and she licked them as she stared back. He wanted nothing more than to push her against the table behind them and rip her jeans off and gorge himself on her essence, but that would've been going a bit too far.

She smiled as if she could read his mind. "Bucatini," she said. "I also picked up a bottle of red wine. Meiomi...it's a pinot noir that's popular northeast of us. I think you'll like it."

"I'm sure I will," Storm said, doing his best to bring his body under control.

Jane nodded and started to take a step back, but Storm stopped her. He liked her plastered up against him. Liked that he could see her hard nipples under her pink shirt. "I've never felt like that before," he told her.

She tilted her head in question.

"Like if I didn't get inside you in ten seconds, I'd lose my fucking mind," he said. Storm knew he was being crude, but he couldn't stop long enough to try to find more polite words. "I don't know what it is about you, but you've crawled under my skin, and I don't want you to leave," he admitted.

"It's been a long time for me," Jane replied. "I've weathered a lot of storms in my personal life, but I honestly didn't expect them to last as long as they have."

He recognized the line from their favorite movie, but didn't interrupt.

"But now that I'm finally seeing the light, that Rose and I have some semblance of a normal relationship again, I'm ready to see if I can be selfish and concentrate on me for a while."

"So I'm what...some sort of liberation for you?" Storm asked, confused.

"No!" she said immediately. "That's not what I meant. I had the thought that I'd date men who wouldn't want anything serious. To experience a kind of sex I hadn't ever had. But then I saw you...and that was that. I didn't want anyone else. How could I when you were everything I'd ever wanted in my life? Handsome, considerate, successful, respected, funny... I told myself that you were out of my league. That you'd never notice someone like me. But then you did, and I was on top of the world. Though I'm worried I won't live up to any expectations you have when it comes to the bedroom."

Storm couldn't help it—he laughed.

When Jane stiffened, he shook his head. "I'm not laughing at you, Jane, I'm laughing because there's no way in hell you can let me down. That kiss we shared was the hottest thing I've ever experienced in my life. And for the record, I haven't been with anyone in a really long time either. I have no doubt we'll be combustible when we get together, but there's no pressure. I didn't come over here expecting you to sleep with me. I was looking forward to spending more time with you. To spending as much of my forty-eight hours' downtime with you as possible. Talking, laughing, eating, watching TV. That's it."

"So you don't want to sleep with me?" she asked, her brows furrowing.

"Oh, I want to," he said quickly. "But I don't *expect* to. How fast things go between us is up to you. But know this...when I do take you to bed, I'm going to want it all from you. No hiding in the dark under the covers. I want the lights on, you spread open for me so I can look my fill. You're beautiful, and I have a feeling I'm never going to get enough."

He loved the blush that formed on her face, but more than that, he loved that she obviously craved to be with him in the same way.

"Okay," she said after a moment.

"Okay," he agreed. "Now, how about we eat before my stomach

makes its disapproval known again over how little I've fed it today."

Jane nodded, and he allowed her to pull away. He followed her into the kitchen and helped her dish up their meals. When they sat down to eat, it was surprisingly comfortable. There was no uneasiness because of their conversation. She laughed with him and happily shared her branzino, just as she snuck pieces of his bucatini.

They talked about nothing and everything. How she liked to collect pretty shells she found on the beaches around the base, how he had a thing for comfortable socks…he hated wearing scratchy socks, or having the poorly placed seams rub his toes the wrong way.

By the time they did the dishes and settled on her couch to watch a *Seinfeld* rerun, Storm felt even more like he'd known Jane forever. Being with her felt right, as if his favorite old pair of socks had magically been restored to their fluffiness and newness once again.

He only wished he'd found her years earlier, so they'd have had more time to be together.

Chapter Seven

Jane had her head on Storm's shoulder and was as comfortable as she could ever remember being. It had taken her forever to get to this point with her ex. Yes, she'd been a teenager, but she hadn't let him kiss her like Storm had until they'd known each other for months.

It was insane. She was a grown-ass woman who couldn't keep carnal thoughts out of her head, of going to her knees in front of Storm and drawing his zipper down and taking him in her mouth right then and there. She hadn't even thought that she *liked* sex all that much until she'd started fantasizing about him. And when he finally kissed her, she'd gone a little crazy, wanting to touch him from head to toe. Thank God his stomach had growled and brought her back to her senses.

But now, they were sitting on her couch watching Jerry Seinfeld try to guess his girlfriend's name, which he knew rhymed with a body part, and all she could think about was jumping Storm.

She loved that he was being a gentleman and not trying to rush her, but Jane realized she *wanted* to be rushed. Would he think she was too aggressive if she initiated more than just snuggling?

"What are you thinking about so hard over there?" Storm asked. "And don't tell me it's the show, because while Jerry thinking his girlfriend's name is Mulva is funny, it's not deep enough for you to have this furrow in your brows." He ran a fingertip over her forehead, and Jane shivered slightly at the feel of his callused fingertip against her skin.

"I don't want you to think badly of me," Jane said.

"Nothing you say would make me think badly of you," he reassured her.

Taking a deep breath and deciding to just say what was on her mind, Jane blurted, "I want you."

To Storm's credit, his expression didn't change. But she did see his pupils dilate.

He took a deep breath and shifted next to her, putting his finger under her chin so she couldn't look away from him. "Brave," he muttered. Then said louder, "I want you too. Badly. But if at any time you change your mind, all you have to do is tell me, and that'll be that."

"I won't change my mind," Jane assured him.

"Even so. I don't want to do anything that'll make you uncomfortable. You get second thoughts, or start to feel awkward, just say the word."

"Okay. Same goes for you," she told him.

Storm tilted his head in question.

"What? I know the media concentrates on women having the right to say no, but men have that right too. Just because I want to have sex doesn't mean *you* do."

Storm chuckled and dropped his finger from her chin. "I want to," he said earnestly.

Then his finger traced the neckline of the V-neck blouse she was wearing, and his eyes lowered as his finger moved...

Jane shivered and felt her nipples harden. She knew he could see her physical reaction to his touch, because he licked his lips and inhaled deeply. She had a feeling if things got started here on her couch, she wasn't going to want to move to her bed later, so without a word, she stood and held out her hand.

Storm immediately took hold and followed her out of the room and into the short hallway that led to the two bedrooms. Jane would've been embarrassed about the state of her room—she wasn't exactly a neatnik—but the one time she looked back at Storm, his eyes were glued to her ass, so she didn't think he would even notice her clutter.

She led him to the side of her full-size bed. It had always been big enough for her, but now that he would be joining her in it, she wondered if he'd think it was too small.

Refusing to feel bad about the way she lived—it hadn't been easy or cheap being a single mother—Jane let go of Storm's hand long enough to open a drawer in a small table next to her bed. She pulled out the box of condoms she'd bought earlier that week, when she'd been wishful thinking. "I hope this isn't a problem."

Storm immediately shook his head. "I'm clean. I told you it's been a while since I've been with anyone, and I wasn't lying about that. But I'm more than okay with using protection. I'd never do anything to put you at risk."

The topic was a bit embarrassing, but she was an adult, and if she was going to do adult things like have sex, she had to be mature enough to talk about stuff like protection. "I'm clean too, and it's not likely I'd get pregnant, but I don't want to chance it."

"I don't blame you," Storm said, taking the box out of her hand and placing it on the bedside table. He wrapped a hand around her neck and intertwined his fingers in her hair, forcing her head back a bit. That tiny show of control made her shiver in excitement. "I'd never risk your health. Ever," he said evenly. "But," he continued, "I can't deny that the thought of being inside you bare is a hell of a turn-on. If things between us work out, which I'm counting on, we'll have to see what we can do to make that happen."

"Yes," Jane whispered, the thought of him taking her bare turning her on even more.

"Any other concerns you want to bring up?" Storm asked.

"No."

Storm tightened his hand in her hair for just a moment, then nodded and released her. He stepped back and brought his hands to the hem of his shirt, lifting it up and over his head in one quick movement.

Jane swallowed hard and licked her lips in anticipation. Storm was *built*. She'd seen his body before but hadn't been in the frame of mind to appreciate it. His chest was covered with a light coating of hair, which was sexy as hell, but for now, she was more interested in feeling every one of the muscles she could see bulging in his chest and arms.

Curling her arms around his biceps, she leaned into him and licked his right nipple.

"Damn," Storm said under his breath, covering the back of her head with his large hand, pressing her harder against him.

Smiling, Jane took the hint and drew his nipple into her mouth, sucking hard. He groaned, and his hand tightened in her hair.

Jane switched to the other nipple and couldn't help but feel completely empowered by his unrestrained reaction to her mouth on him. Glancing down, she could see his cock pushing against the fly of his jeans.

She'd never been too concerned about the size of a man before, believing what he could *do* with his appendage was more important, but she couldn't help being impressed by what Storm was packing.

The grip on her hair got tighter, and she let Storm pull her head away from his body. "Enough," he said in a low, gravelly voice. "I need to see you. I've fantasized about you standing in front of me naked...and not because you're hurt this time."

Jane flushed, not wanting to remember when she'd had to strip for him out of necessity. This time it was *her* choice. And she wasn't hacking up a lung from CS gas.

His hand dropped from her head as she stepped back and reached for the button on her jeans. She undid it and pushed the denim down her legs, stepping out of it. She reached under her shirt and undid the clasp of her strapless bra, smiling as Storm eyed what he could see of her legs. She dropped her bra and stood up straight. She reached for the bottom of her shirt, but he stopped her.

"Let me," he said quietly.

Nodding, Jane lowered her hands.

Storm grasped the edge of her shirt, and she felt his fingers brush against her sides. She sucked in her stomach as best she could, wishing she was in better shape for him. Wished her belly wasn't so big and that her thighs were more toned. Her butt had *always* been big, and she worried that he'd be turned off by it.

By the time all her insecurities ran through her brain, Storm had gripped the material of her blouse and raised it up and over her head. She raised her arms to assist, then was standing in front of him in nothing but the pair of black cotton underwear she'd put on earlier.

"Beautiful," Storm breathed as he simply stared. His hands went back to resting on her hips, but he didn't move otherwise.

Fidgeting, Jane said, "I'm not twenty-three anymore."

Storm snorted. "Thank God," he told her. "Turn."

Blinking in surprise, Jane asked, "What?"

"Turn around. I want to see your ass."

Holding her breath, Jane did as he asked, loving how he didn't take his hands off her as she turned and faced her bed.

"Damn. Better than my fantasies," Storm told her.

She looked over her shoulder and saw that his eyes were glued to the butt she'd thought too big and flabby almost her entire life.

Then he crouched behind her and took the globes of her ass in his hands and squeezed.

Squeaking in surprise, Jane stumbled and caught herself on her mattress, which left her bending over slightly.

"Fuck yeah," Storm murmured, and Jane felt his fingers brush against the soaking-wet gusset of her panties.

With anyone else, she might've been embarrassed, but with the way Storm was crouched behind her, she could clearly see his erection. The second she had the thought, one of his hands went to the button and zipper on his jeans and undid them. He groaned in relief, then brought his hand back to her ass.

"You're gorgeous," he told her, not taking his eyes from her body.

"I could lose some weight," she said softly.

"No fucking way," he told her firmly.

"But you're so in shape. So...hard," she protested.

"I am." He grinned. "But that doesn't mean that's how I appreciate my women. I like *soft*," he told her. "I can't wait to feel your curves against me. Surrounding me. Holding me."

His words were seducing her even more than the feel of his hands on her body.

He applied slight pressure on her hips, indicating that he wanted her to turn around for him. Jane did, and then she was looking down at him, still crouched in front of her. She could see the head of his cock peeking out through the slit in the boxers he was wearing. Licking her lips, she had the sudden desire to see more of him. All of him.

But he had other ideas. He hooked his fingers in the waistband of her panties and looked up. "May I?" he asked.

Jane nodded.

Then he slowly drew the cotton down over her hips and thighs. She kicked them away when they fell to the carpet at her feet—and then she was naked in front of Storm. The man she'd crushed on for ages. She would've been nervous, but the look of utter lust on his face made all her worries drain away.

"Fuck," he whispered, then leaned forward and nuzzled the crease where her leg met her hip.

Jane whimpered. She knew she was soaking wet, and she was anxious to have his hands all over her. "Storm," she begged.

"What?" he asked, not taking his eyes from between her legs.

"Touch me."

"I am," he said. "You smell so damn good."

Jane's heart rate was off the charts, and she wanted to do more than just look at the amazingly handsome man at her feet. She sat on the mattress suddenly and scooted backward. Pushing the comforter and sheet down, she lay back, propping herself up on her elbows. "I'm not sure why I'm the only one naked here," she managed to say in a semi-normal tone.

Getting the hint, Storm shoved his jeans and boxers down and off and was lying half on top of her on the bed before she could take a full breath. Jane felt his hard cock against her thigh and, without thought, moved a hand down to grasp him.

He grunted and thrust into her grip once before reaching down and grabbing her wrist. He brought her hand up and over her head, claiming the other one in the process. Jane grinned at him.

"Minx," he said with a chuckle. "Any more of that, and I'd lose it, and the fun would be over before it began."

"Would it?" she asked.

"I'm not a young man anymore," he told her with a lack of self-recrimination. "And as I said, it's been a long time since I've done this. The last thing I want is to spill myself anywhere but inside that condom when I'm deep inside your hot, wet body. So until then, I'm gonna need you to keep your hands to yourself."

Jane mock-pouted. "What fun is that?"

"Oh, we're gonna have fun," Storm countered.

"I can't touch you at all?" Jane asked, feeling disappointed.

He studied her for a second. "You want to?"

"Yes," she told him honestly.

"For now, you can touch me anywhere but my dick. I'm serious when I say all it'll take is a few strokes from you to send me over the edge."

Jane shivered. She liked the feeling of power that gave her. A lot. "Okay."

"Okay," Storm agreed. "Let me know if I do something you don't like."

And that was the only warning she got before he was easing down her body. When his head reached her chest, one hand plumped up her breast, and he took her nipple into his mouth.

If Jane thought he'd go slow and easy, she was wrong. Very wrong. He suckled against her so hard, she felt the tugging in her womb. Arching her back, Jane clamped on to his biceps and held on for dear life.

She rocked in his grip until he had to use one hand to hold her hip still. Then he switched to the other side, giving that nipple the same treatment as the first. Jane whimpered, loving the pleasure/pain his mouth was giving her. She'd never thought her breasts were that sensitive, but she'd never had someone treat them the way Storm was. She wanted him to stop, yet wanted him to keep going. It was confusing and erotic as hell.

With a pop, he took his mouth off her and grinned when she sighed. "Holy shit, Storm."

"Feel good?" he asked.

"Oh yeah."

He nodded in satisfaction, then scooted farther down her body.

Jane knew she shouldn't feel nervous. She'd given and received oral sex in the past, but for some reason, the way Storm was looking at her as if she was his next meal made her uneasy.

"Storm?"

"Yeah, baby?" he asked.

She shivered at hearing the endearment. "Go easy," she pleaded.

For a second she thought he was going to ignore her, but then he nodded. It was just a dip of his chin, but she relaxed. He nudged her legs farther apart. "More," he ordered.

Jane put her feet flat on the bed and dropped her knees out. Storm immediately shoved his shoulders between her thighs, and she felt the burn on her inner muscles. She would be sore tomorrow but was looking forward to the delicious ache.

One hand rested on her belly, holding her down, and the fingertips on the other brushed over her soaked folds. "So fucking beautiful," he murmured before his head dropped.

Jane tensed, ready for anything, but when his tongue lightly licked up her labia, she shuddered in ecstasy and relaxed completely.

What came next was twenty minutes of Storm worshiping her sex until she was writhing and begging him for more. To touch her harder, to suck on her. She loved the feel of him being sweet and easy, but she needed more.

Storm lifted his head, and Jane saw her juices glistening on his chin. "Hold on," he told her.

"To what?" Jane asked.

"To me." Then Storm lowered his head once more—and Jane could tell immediately that he was done being slow and gentle. One finger eased inside her channel, and he wrapped his lips around her clit. He sucked, using his tongue like a mini-vibrator to lash against her ultra-sensitive bundle of nerves. The finger that was inside her curved and pressed against her G-spot.

And just like that, Jane knew she was going to come. Hard.

"Storm!" she cried out even as her stomach muscles clenched and she curled upward. One hand clutched the hair on top of his head and the other gripped the wrist of the hand still resting on her belly.

He moaned against her clit, and that was all it took. She went flying over the edge with an orgasm so intense, she saw little black dots float in front of her eyes. She felt Storm add another finger inside her, and he fucked her hard, even as his lips stayed suctioned over her clit and she bucked and thrashed under him.

Finally, she croaked, "No more, too sensitive!" as his ministrations turned painful. He immediately lifted his head and removed his fingers. But he didn't move from between her legs. Instead, he immediately began lapping at the juices he'd called forth from her body. Lazily, he ran his tongue up her lips, over and over, obviously enjoying the fruit of his labors.

When she felt completely wrung out, Jane slumped back onto the mattress, breathing hard, as if she'd just run a marathon.

When Storm moved from between her legs, she didn't have the strength to close them. He came up and over her on his hands and knees and reached over to the table. He opened the box of condoms and within seconds had rolled one down his very impressive cock.

"Can I touch you now?" she asked.

He hesitated, but nodded.

He was kneeling between her legs, and Jane reached down and grasped his throbbing erection. He was big. Bigger than anyone she'd ever been with, but that thought excited rather than frightened her. She'd take him and hopefully make him feel as good as he'd just made her feel.

"Ready?" Storm asked as he nudged her legs apart once more.

Jane nodded and brought one leg up and curled it around his thigh. He took hold of his dick and ran the head through her wet folds. It felt good.

He obviously thought so too, because the veins in the sides of his neck bulged, and he groaned.

"This is gonna be fast," he warned her.

"Okay," she agreed.

Then Storm slowly, ever so slowly, pushed his length inside her until she could feel his balls pressed up against her ass. Then he put a hand under her and lifted her up and into him even farther. She could feel him stretching her from the inside out, but it didn't hurt.

"Damn, you feel amazing," Storm said, his eyes boring into hers.

"You too," she said.

Then he surprised the hell out of her by sitting back on his heels and hauling her ass onto his thighs.

"What are you doing?" she asked.

"As I said, the second I start thrusting inside your insanely hot body, I'm going to go off like a rocket. I want you to come again before I do."

Jane hadn't ever orgasmed from sex alone. It had always taken direct stimulation on her clit to make that happen, and most men didn't have the wherewithal to make sure she was enjoying herself while they were in the middle of sex.

"It's fine," Jane tried to reassure him. "Trust me, you already made me come harder than I can ever remember coming in my life."

"Good," he said with satisfaction. "This time I want to feel it against my cock."

Then he rested his thumb on her still extremely sensitive clit and pressed.

"Damn!" Jane exclaimed as she jerked in his grasp.

"You're so slick," he said as he played with her. "And you tasted so good. I can't wait to get my mouth on you again. You're going to be sore with how much I want to eat you out."

His words were filthy but hot as hell. No one had ever talked to her that way, and Jane liked it. She'd just come, but she felt another orgasm welling up inside her already.

"That's it. I can feel you twitching against me. It feels amazing. Like nothing I've experienced before. Keep going. Come on my dick, Jane...squeeze me."

As if she was programmed to do exactly what he ordered, amazingly, Jane felt herself exploding once more.

"Oh yeah, shit, that's so fucking good. You're rippling against me... Damn, I can't hold back. Hang on, baby," Storm told her. Then he moved until he was on his knees once more and began pounding into her body.

Jane's orgasm seemed to go on and on, kept alive by the feel of Storm's big cock sliding in and out of her, awakening nerves that hadn't been stimulated in years.

"I'm gonna want to take you from behind soon, baby. Watch that gorgeous ass shake and shimmy as I fuck you. God, you're so beautiful…"

For the first time in her life, Jane *felt* beautiful. With this virile and handsome man taking his pleasure from her body, looking at her with clear lust and affection in his eyes. She wanted to give him so much. Anything he wanted, she'd give him, because she knew he'd return the pleasure to her tenfold.

"Oh shit, not yet," Storm said, but it was too late. He shoved himself inside her as far as he could go, let his head drop back, and his entire body shook as he orgasmed.

Jane's hands caressed his arms as he propped himself over her, and after a long moment, he groaned and practically collapsed on top of her.

"That's it. I'm dead. You killed me," he exclaimed, being sure not to crush her as he lay against her.

"Get busy livin' or get busy dyin'," she quipped.

A startled laugh escaped him, and his cock slipped out of her body with the movement.

"Damn," he said in disappointment.

Jane was disappointed too, but when Storm rolled over and pulled her into his arms, she couldn't complain. Her arms were trapped between them, and they were both a bit sweaty from their lovemaking, but Jane didn't care. She nuzzled his neck, and her fingertips caressed his chest where they rested against him.

"You all right?" he asked quietly.

"Oh yeah," she said on a sigh.

"Thank you," Storm told her.

"I think that's my line," Jane said.

But Storm didn't even grin. "Thank you for trusting me with your body. For giving me the best gift I've gotten in a very long damn time."

"You're welcome. Are you staying?"

At that, Storm raised his head to look at her.

Jane bravely met his eyes. "I mean, I want you to, but I don't know what the rules are here."

"Rules?" he asked.

"Yeah, dating rules. I'm out of practice."

"I don't give a shit about what other people do," Storm said firmly. "If you'll let me stay, I want to stay. I can't think of anything better than spending all of my forty-eight-hour leave with you. Not just the daylight hours."

Jane knew she had a goofy grin on her face, but she couldn't help it. "I'm sure you'll need to go home and get clothes and whatnot at some point."

"I will," he agreed. "And if you're open to it, you can pack a bag and come with me. I'll make dinner tomorrow night, and you can spend the night in *my* bed."

"How did this happen?" Jane asked, more to herself than Storm.

"You knocked me off my feet with your bravery and selflessness," he told her seriously. "Then I realized how beautiful, smart, and funny you were. I was a goner."

Jane rolled her eyes.

"I'm serious," he said. "You've everything a man could want. I'm just sorry I didn't see what was right in front of my face earlier."

"Me too," she admitted.

"But I'm here now…and I'm not going anywhere."

Jane liked that a hell of a lot. She opened her mouth to tell him so, but yawned instead.

Storm chuckled. "Tired?"

"Yeah. It's been a hell of a long two weeks. Not to mention the two orgasms I had tonight."

He grinned. "You were spectacular," he praised. "I need to take care of this condom, then we'll sleep."

"Okay," she agreed and sighed in contentment when he leaned over, kissed her forehead, then climbed out of her bed. She straightened the covers and pillows while he was gone and didn't bother to hide the fact she was ogling him when he walked back to bed completely naked.

"Like what you see?" he asked with a smile as he crawled under the covers and pulled her into him.

"Duh," she replied returning his grin.

"Me too," he told her as his hand caressed over her ass cheeks under the covers.

Jane snuggled into the man at her side and sighed in happiness. One moment she was thanking her lucky stars that Storm had somehow noticed her, and the next she was in a deep, contented sleep.

Chapter Eight

By the time Sunday night came around, Storm already knew he was completely head over heels for Jane. He didn't feel any of the angst he occasionally felt when he spent time with some of the women he'd dated in the past. He hadn't constantly been looking at his watch to see when he could extricate himself, and when it came time for her to leave, he was genuinely disappointed.

While the sex had been amazing, that wasn't the main reason why he was so attracted. He simply enjoyed being around her. She didn't complain about every little thing. She was appreciative of the smallest things he, and others, did for her. Like when they'd gone to the grocery store and the cashier had given her a coupon someone else had left. Anyone watching would've thought the woman had saved Jane a hundred bucks rather than just fifty cents.

He also liked that Jane was somewhat shy. Storm had spent his entire life as a protector, and he enjoyed the role. So when a man bumped into Jane so hard she nearly fell on her ass, he was happy to jump to her defense.

Storm couldn't believe that he'd known Jane as long as he had without realizing what a great person she was. He felt stupid and disgusted with himself. With her shyness, however, he knew she never would've made the first move, and he thanked his lucky stars he'd finally seen the gem that was right under his nose.

"What do you have on tap for the week?" she asked as they stood in the parking lot of his townhouse complex next to her older model black Toyota Camry.

"Meetings, research, and trying to help Dag plow through court-martial records," he told her. "He said he didn't need help, but I want this done. Partly because he's my friend, and I hate that he could be in danger, but also because the last thing I want is you getting any more caught up in this than you already are."

"But you're already so busy," she said.

"I am, but *I'm* always doing meetings and research, so it's not a big deal."

Jane wrinkled her nose adorably. "That doesn't sound fun."

Storm chuckled. "It's not bad. I'm used to it."

She nodded.

Then something occurred to him. "This coming weekend there's a SEAL get-together on the beach. Want to come with me?"

Jane blinked in surprise. "Really?"

After their weekend together, it kinda irritated him that she was so surprised he'd ask. "Yeah, really."

She obviously realized that she'd upset him as her hand came up and rested on his chest, right over his heart. She petted him as if he were a dangerous animal that needed soothing. "I just...this thing between us is new, and I wasn't sure if you wanted to advertise to those we worked with about it...well, other than the few people who already know."

Storm frowned. "We aren't breaking any rules. You aren't in the Navy, so it's not fraternization."

"I know," she said quickly, "But...I'd hate for things to get weird if..." Her voice trailed off.

Storm stepped forward and crowded her until she'd backed up against her car.

"Storm?"

"Don't think about us breaking up before we even get started," he growled.

"I'm not. I mean, it's just...you're you, and I'm me."

"What the hell does that mean?" he asked.

Jane bit her lip and looked up at him in consternation.

Storm took a deep breath and framed her face with his hands. He leaned down and rested his forehead against hers. "I like you, Jane. A hell of a lot. I don't know much about the obvious losers you've dated in the past, but not one of my coworkers or SEALs will think we're mismatched.

Hell, they'll probably take me aside and warn me I better not be fucking with you."

"I like you too," she whispered. "I'm just terrified you're going to wake up and wonder what the hell you're doing with me. I've got a grown daughter who I'm not on the best of terms with, even though it's gotten better in the last year or so. I'm approaching middle age, and while I make enough to keep a roof over my head, I'm not exactly raking in the bucks."

He drew back and looked her in the eyes. "And you're genuinely nice, you go out of your way to help anyone however you can, you work hard and aren't a freeloader. You kiss like an angel and you're uninhibited in bed...and you make me feel like the luckiest man on earth."

He smiled as she blushed adorably.

"And you still blush when I compliment you," he finished. "Please say you'll come with me. I want to show you off to everyone. Show you how welcoming the SEAL community can be."

"Okay," she whispered.

"Okay," he echoed. "Jane?"

"Yeah?" she asked.

"I had a really great weekend. I loved hanging out with you, learning how you take your coffee, watching you get ready in the morning...the last forty-eight hours have been some of the best in my life, and I'm not just saying that."

"Me too," she agreed. "I can't believe you got the ratio of cream and sweetener for my coffee right after watching me make my first cup," she teased. "I don't think my ex ever got it right, even after a decade of being married."

"I know this is fast, but I wouldn't be opposed to you staying over during the week," Storm told her. When her eyes widened in surprise, he quickly added, "I'm not asking you to move in, it's way too soon for that, but I've slept better this weekend than I have in a very long time, and I would certainly enjoy having dinner with you more often, and waking up with you by my side."

"It must've been a *really* long time since you'd had sex," she teased.

Storm didn't take offense. He'd even surprised himself with the offer for her to stay over, and he could just imagine what she was thinking. "I won't deny that sex with you is more meaningful than with anyone I've ever slept with, but that wasn't what I was implying. I just...coming home to an empty townhouse doesn't hold any appeal any longer. Not after spending the last two days with you, hearing your laughter, watching you read on my couch as I get some research work done. I just like having you around and wouldn't mind spending as much time with you as possible...outside the bedroom. I'm not saying I don't want to be intimate with you, but I'm not twenty-two anymore...I don't need or want sex every night."

Storm held his breath waiting for her response. "I'd like that," she said softly.

He beamed, and his shoulders relaxed. Storm hadn't realized how tense he'd become. "Good. We'll figure it out as the week goes on then."

"Okay."

"But plan on staying over Friday night for sure. The SEAL get-together is on Saturday and we'll need to go shopping to pick up some watermelon before we head over there."

"Will there be a lot of people?" she asked tentatively.

Storm didn't want to freak her out, but he wasn't going to lie to her either. "Yeah, baby, there will. You know there are a lot of SEAL teams on the base, and this beach party is for their families too. I can't wait to introduce you to Wolf and his team and all their families, as well as Rocco and his team and families too."

Jane bit her lip again, and Storm couldn't help leaning down and licking where she'd nervously bitten herself. "It'll be fine. *You'll* be fine."

"You aren't just going to leave me when we get there, are you?" she asked after a moment. "I mean, I'm aware that you'll know everyone and will want to talk to them, but I don't do great in big groups when I don't know anyone."

"I'd never do that," he told her honestly. "But I guarantee that you'll know more people than you think. Trust me not to bring you somewhere then desert you."

She sighed. "I do."

She didn't. Not yet, but Storm would do whatever he could to put her at ease and to make her trust him. They were still getting to know each other, and the more time they spent together, the more she'd realize that he wasn't her ex. That he wasn't going to treat her like shit and leave her to fend for herself. She'd been doing that for far too long. While she'd more than proven she was independent and wouldn't fall apart if she had to do shit on her own, he wanted to show her that she was no longer alone. That she could lean on him.

"Drive safe going home," he told her quietly. "Text or call me when you're inside safe and sound, okay?"

"I will," she agreed. Then she smiled. "It's nice to have someone be worried about me. It's been a very long time."

"Get used to it," Storm warned her. "It might be nice now, but you might get irritated and sick of me being overprotective."

"I doubt it," she told him. "I mean, when you haven't ever had that, it feels pretty damn good. As long as you don't get crazy and start tracking my every movement like a psycho stalker, I'm okay with you wanting to make sure I'm safe."

Storm leaned in and kissed her. It seemed like forever since he'd had his lips on hers, but in reality it had only been about twenty minutes…right before they'd left his townhouse. She immediately opened for him, and he loved how receptive she was.

Reluctantly, he pulled back and kissed her on the forehead one more time before stepping back and opening her door. He waited until she was seated and had her safety belt on before leaning down and kissing her once more, briefly this time. "Drive safe."

Jane nodded at him and smiled as he closed her door. She waved at him, and he gave her a chin lift in return. He stood in the parking lot and watched until he couldn't see her taillights anymore. Then he took a deep breath and turned to walk back to his front door.

Storm was somewhat surprised at how empty his place felt when he reentered. He'd lived alone a very long time, but after only two days, Jane had filled his home with laughter and companionship.

It was true, when the right person came along…you just knew it. Jane filled all the lonely holes deep within him he'd refused to acknowledge. He didn't regret asking her to consider spending more nights with him. He couldn't think of anything better than coming home from a long day of work to her. He didn't need dinner on the table, or the house cleaned…he just needed her to talk to. Laugh with. Snuggle with.

* * * *

On Wednesday afternoon, Jane looked down at her phone during one of her breaks and smiled when she saw she had a text from Storm.

Storm: It's been three nights. Any chance you'd consider coming over tonight?

She typed out a short but heartfelt response.

Jane: Yes!

His reply came almost immediately, as if he'd been waiting for her to text him back.

> *Storm: Thank God. I should get off around five-thirty. Come over anytime after six.*
> *Jane: Okay. I need to go home and get my things, but barring any disasters here at work, I should be there by six-thirty.*
> *Storm: Sounds perfect. I'll start dinner.*
> *Jane: What're we having?*
> *Storm: I went home at lunch and put a pot roast in the Crock-Pot. I hope that's all right.*
> *Jane: Yum!*
> *Storm: You're easy to please.*
> *Jane: Actually, I'm not. I'm picky in my taste in men, I don't like seafood, and kale goes on my gross list.*
> *Storm: Crosses kale off list for dinner tonight.*
> *Jane: Shut up.*
> *Storm: :)*
> *Storm: I'm looking forward to seeing you. I feel like it's been forever since I saw you last.*
> *Jane: You saw me this morning when I brought your mail up.*
> *Storm: Like I said, forever.*

Jane sighed in contentment. She'd sorta thought Storm would be standoffish at work and not very romantic when it came to everyday life, but she'd been wrong. While he didn't bend her over his arm and make out with her while they were on the base, he didn't hesitate to touch her, to kiss her on the cheek, to let her know he was happy to see her.

His text and emails were sweet and somewhat sappy. And when he called, he never hesitated to let her know how pretty he thought she was, how happy he was to talk to her, and how much he missed her. The difference between him and other men she'd dated was night and day. It almost made the way they'd gotten together, with her practically naked after being doused with tear gas, worth it. Almost.

> *Jane: Do you want me to bring anything when I come over tonight?*
> *Storm: Just you.*

Jane: I'm serious. I can pick something up from the store if I need to.
Storm: I AM being serious. Just bring yourself, baby.
Jane: Okay. See you later.
Storm: Can't wait.

Jane put her cell back in her pocket. It was amazing how good Storm made her feel. It scared her but at the same time made her feel decades younger. She'd never expected this. Not at her age.

Taking a deep breath, she got back to work with renewed purpose. She needed to make sure she was finished with sorting the mail on time tonight so she could get home, pack, and head over to Storm's place. Being with him made her realize how lonely she'd really been. She'd worked her ass off to raise Rose, and after she'd left, Jane had spent a lot of time and energy worrying about her…as any good mom would do.

But with every year that passed, and the closer she got to retirement, Jane realized that she had a lot of years left of her life. That she'd be alone if she didn't manage to find someone to spend her golden years with. She would've been content with finding a group of friends, but being with Storm was like a dream come true. She was nervous about the beach party that weekend but decided to do her best to take things as they came. Worrying if people would like her wasn't going to do anything but stress her out.

Knowing she needed to concentrate on work and put Storm and the upcoming night out of her mind, Jane reached for another packet of letters.

* * * *

At six-thirty on the nose, Jane knocked on Storm's door. He opened it almost immediately. He had a huge smile on his face and pulled her into his arms even as he shut the door with his foot.

"Hey," he said.

"Hi," she responded.

Then he kissed her. A long, deep kiss that Jane knew she'd never get tired of. When he lifted his head, he smiled down at her once more, brushing a lock of hair off her forehead. "Damn, it's good to see you. Come on, dinner's almost ready. You've got to be hungry."

Bemused, Jane let him pull her into his house, loving how he kept hold of her hand. Dinner smelled delicious, and she couldn't remember ever being spoiled like this. She loved it.

He pulled her small bag out of her hand and put it by the stairs continuing on toward the kitchen. Within twenty minutes, they were sitting at a small table off the kitchen and Storm was telling her about his day.

"Dag and I reviewed records today and narrowed the list of suspects down to about five."

"That many?" Jane asked in surprise.

"Yeah. There are a lot of good men and women in the Navy, but there are also quite a few who never quite conform. Sometimes they're lazy and want to take the easy way out. Other times they just make a stupid mistake that can't be overlooked and forgiven. We're assuming the bomber is someone who was court-martialed out of the Navy. It might be an erroneous assumption, but we don't think so. Someone has to be upset enough at Dag to blame him for whatever happened to them, and if someone was just given nonjudicial punishment, I don't think they'd be as upset."

"What does NCIS think?" Jane asked.

"They agree. And they're investigating as many of the sailors who were kicked out of the Navy in the last year as they can. Trying to find out where they are now and interviewing new coworkers if possible. It's a slow process. And I know it's frustrating. Are you okay?"

"Me? Yeah, why wouldn't I be?" Jane asked in surprise.

Storm reached over and took her hand in his. "You haven't had any flashbacks or bad moments about what happened to you?"

Jane hesitated. She wanted to say no, that she was fine, but she also didn't want to lie. She settled for shrugging. "Nothing major."

The look of concern on his face made her melt. "I'm sorry, baby. I know it's not a lot, but hopefully it'll help in the long run that you weren't the target."

"I know. That's why I feel stupid about the bad dreams I've had. I was just unlucky enough to be caught in the crossfire, so to speak," she told him.

"Don't feel stupid," Storm said immediately, taking her hand in his. "What happened to you was traumatic. It was unexpected, and you were attacked in your safe space. You're allowed to react badly to that."

Jane nodded. "The dreams aren't horrible. I usually wake up just as the bomb is going off. For a second I can't breathe, remembering how much the tear gas stung, but then I realize that I'm just dreaming and I'm afe."

"You *are* safe," Storm told her.

Jane smiled at him. "Thanks."

He squeezed her hand once more, then let go to finish eating. They alked about nothing important until they were done and continued alking as they sat on the couch afterward. In fact, Jane couldn't emember ever talking this much about nothing with someone else and ot feeling awkward or having any long pauses between topics.

It wasn't until he yawned that she looked at her watch and realized it vas almost ten o'clock. They'd been chatting away for hours. "Holy crap," he exclaimed. "It's late."

Storm chuckled. "So it is. You ready to head up?"

He made it sound so normal. This was only the third time they'd pent the night together, and already it felt as if they'd done it a hundred imes. "Yeah," she told him.

"I'll just make sure everything's tidied up and locked down here. You o on up. I'll be there in a few minutes."

She appreciated him giving her some time to get situated. She felt omfortable with him, but not quite comfortable enough yet to change in ront of him as if she'd done it every day of her life.

She nodded and stood, but Storm grabbed her hand before she could valk off.

"Jane?"

"Yeah?"

"I like this. A lot. You have an open invitation to stay over here as nuch as you want. Feel free to leave some of your things too, to make it asier. Shampoo, nightgown…whatever."

Jane stared at Storm for a heartbeat. "Are you sure?" she asked quietly. "I don't want to wear out my welcome."

Storm stood and ran his finger down her cheek. "I'm more than sure. I feel more relaxed and content with you here."

Now *that* was an awesome compliment.

He brushed his thumb over her lips then stood back. "Go on. I'll be here in a bit."

Nodding, Jane grabbed her bag and headed up the stairs. Upon entering his room, she took a deep breath, loving how it smelled like him. She quickly changed into the boy shorts and T-shirt she liked to wear to oed and got ready in the bathroom. By the time Storm came upstairs, she vas sitting in his bed with her iPad, reading.

He saw her and smiled hugely. "Fuck, I love seeing you there," he muttered then headed for the bathroom. He came back out a few minutes later wearing nothing but a pair of boxers. He turned off the overhead light and climbed in next to her.

"Will it bother you if I read?" she asked.

"No," Storm said immediately. "Does it bother you that I left the bathroom light on? I'm not a fan of pitch-dark rooms. Spent some time in captivity once and ever since, haven't liked the dark."

"Of course not," she told him, feeling her heart break for him. If he wanted to leave all the lights on in the room, she wouldn't complain. How could she after what he'd been through?

"Thanks." Then he plumped his pillow, scooted closer, lay on his side, and draped his arm across her lower stomach.

Jane sat next to him pretending to read for several minutes before she thought he'd fallen asleep. She glanced over at him. His eyes were closed, his mouth was partly open, and he was breathing deeply. She could see the hair on his naked chest and the way his arm muscles bulged even when he was completely relaxed. In short, Storm was absolutely beautiful, and it was hard for Jane to come to terms with the fact that she was in his bed. That he had his arm around her, holding her to him as if he was afraid she'd sneak away when he was sleeping.

Jane loved reading, fell asleep reading most nights. But tonight she didn't need to lose herself in the words of her favorite authors. She was living her own beautiful romance, and she had no idea how she'd gotten there.

Storm wanted her to stay over more? Wanted her to leave some of her things at his place? Hell yes. She was one hundred percent on board with that.

Reaching over, she put her iPad on the table next to her and scooted down on the bed.

"Everything okay?" Storm mumbled, and Jane's heart melted even more. Even half asleep he was worrying about her.

"I'm good. Go back to sleep," she told him gently.

Storm turned onto his back but pulled her toward him. Jane rested her head on his shoulder, and his arm went around her. She snuggled into him and was rewarded with his contented sigh. Her arm rested on his belly, and his free hand lay hot and heavy on top of her forearm.

They were plastered together—and she'd never been more comfortable.

"Hopefully you won't have nightmares sleeping in my arms, but if ou do, I'm here," he told her quietly, then turned and kissed her orehead. Jane swore he was snoring seconds later, but it didn't matter if 1e'd been cognizant of what he'd said or not. She'd treasure his caring vords and actions forever.

She had a feeling Storm had just ruined her for sleeping alone in her double bed. Closing her eyes, Jane sighed in contentment. Within econds, she was dead to the world.

* * * *

Storm woke first the next morning, and it only took a second or two o remember that Jane had stayed the night. The light from the bathroom lluminated the room enough for him to see her. She was currently leeping on her side next to him. He recalled pulling her into his arms the 1ight before, but obviously sometime during the night, they'd both hifted. But what had his heart beating faster was the fact that, while lying 1ext to him, she'd reached out in her sleep to touch him. Her hand was esting on his forearm and the slight weight felt like a brand. One he liked 1 hell of a lot.

How long he lay there watching Jane sleep Storm didn't know. It was till dark outside, but his internal clock told him his alarm would be going off soon. They both had to get to work, but he knew he'd treasure this noment for a long time. He hoped he never took it for granted, the peace ind serenity he got from having Jane by his side. He didn't feel anxious around her, except for her safety.

The second his alarm blared, Storm reached out a hand to shut it off, then turned back to Jane. Her eyes were now open, and she was staring at him.

"Good morning," he said softly.

"Morning," she returned.

He loved the sleepiness he saw in her brown eyes. He wouldn't mind seeing it every morning for the rest of his life…

That thought should've scared the hell out of him, but instead it merely felt right.

"Sleep well?" he asked.

"Better than I have in a very long time…not including last weekend." Storm smiled. "You want to shower first?" he asked.

"Yeah. You take two-point-three seconds to shower and it takes me longer to get ready," Jane said without any heat in her tone.

It was true. He'd learned to take very short showers and hadn't been able to break the habit. "I'll go down and start the coffee while you're showering. You want toast?"

"Please," she said.

When he started to roll out of the bed, her hand tightened on his arm. "Storm?"

He turned back to her. "Yeah, baby?"

"Were you serious last night?"

"About what?"

"About me staying over more?"

"One hundred percent," he replied.

"Good. Because I'm thinking there's nothing I'd like more than to fall asleep in your arms and wake up to see you smiling at me. I feel like I've waited my whole life for you."

Storm swore he could feel his heart swell three times its normal size...kinda like the Grinch's did in the famous story. He leaned over and kissed Jane on the lips. Not pushing to deepen the kiss, but letting her know that her words meant the world to him. "I feel the same," he told her quietly.

Then before he did something that would make them both late for work, he climbed out of bed and headed for the bathroom. After a quick pit stop, and then putting on a pair of cotton pants, he headed for the doorway. He looked back and saw Jane walking toward the bathroom. The boy shorts she was wearing had ridden up, and he could see the round cheeks of her ass sticking out the bottom. And just like that, he was hard.

Groaning quietly, Storm forced himself to exit his room and head for the kitchen. He'd never lived with a woman before, not once in his forty-seven years, but he was definitely seeing the appeal at the moment. But only because it was Jane. He knew she thought she wasn't skinny enough, didn't have the right job...but to him, she was perfect.

They had no time for anything sexual this morning, but on Friday night, all bets were off. He couldn't wait.

* * * *

Jane headed out of Storm's townhouse with him and toward the parking lot.

"We should just go to the base together," he told her.

Jane shook her head. "I love staying with you, but I need my car," he told him. "Sometimes I do errands over my lunch break, and I know you sometimes need to leave base too. It's more practical to drive separately."

She thought it was cute the way Storm scowled. "I know you're right, but I feel cheated out of your presence for even the ten minutes it takes to get to the base."

Jane laughed. "I think we'll survive."

He put a hand on her arm and turned her to face him. "What have you done to me?" he asked.

"The same thing you've done to me," she returned.

"I mean it. Two weeks ago I couldn't think about anything other than work. I lived and breathed it and dreaded coming home. Now I think about you constantly throughout the day. When my phone vibrates with a text, I can't help but think it might be from you, and I get excited. I've been thinking about ways to experiment with food to make things that I think you might enjoy. I swear...I hadn't truly been living until I met you."

Damn. That was the best compliment Jane had ever received. "I feel the same way," she told him.

Storm took a big breath. "Okay, you're right. It's better if we have our own transportation, but that doesn't mean I like it."

She laughed.

"I'll follow you. Be safe."

"I will," she told him.

It was still dark outside, since the sun hadn't quite begun to rise yet. She'd always been startled how it could be dark one moment and then light the next. The sun seemed to sprint up into the sky once it finally woke up.

Storm leaned in and kissed her. It was a long, deep kiss that had Jane's toes curling in her shoes. "I'll walk you in when we get to our building."

"Okay," she agreed easily.

He kissed her once more, a brief kiss that time but no less powerful, then turned and headed for his car.

Jane unlocked her own reliable Camry and climbed inside. She put her overnight bag on the passenger seat, now quite a bit lighter as she'd left her toiletries, her sleep outfit, and the clothes she'd worn yesterday inside Storm's townhouse. It had felt like a big step, and she couldn't help standing in his closet and staring at her things mixed with his in his hamper. Yes, they'd moved fast, but things between them felt right. She wasn't in her twenties anymore. She knew what she wanted—and what she wanted was Storm.

Smiling to herself, she started the engine and headed for the exit. Looking in her rearview mirror, she saw the headlights from Storm's VW Golf behind her. Even though it was early, and she had a long day ahead of her, Jane had never felt more awake and energized than she did right at that moment.

Chapter Nine

Jane nervously walked next to Storm as they headed for the beach on the following Saturday. They were late, but Jane wasn't as worried as she might've been. Storm had kept her up way past her bedtime the night before, and she wasn't complaining.

He'd worshiped her body, going down on her and giving her two bone-melting orgasms before he'd encouraged her to get up on her hands and knees. He'd run his hands over her ass, telling her that he'd fantasized about taking her from behind before proceeding to do just that.

Jane had had sex in that position before, but she'd always felt self-conscious about it. She knew her butt was big. No matter how hard she tried to lose weight—which wasn't very hard, if she was being honest—she'd never been able to lose it from her butt. But last night, Storm had made her promise to never lose her ass, swearing that he loved it too much.

He'd taken her hard and fast, even pushing her down to her elbows at one point as he worshiped her butt while he fucked her. She'd felt more cherished than she might've expected while being taken from behind. Storm never let her think for a second that he didn't know it was *her* he was fucking. He said her name often and encouraged her to look back at him as much as she was comfortable with. In short, he was absolutely perfect, and they'd both slept like the dead, waking up late and not even caring.

But the closer they got to the beach and the more people Jane saw, the more she regretted being fashionably late. The second they stepped foot on the beach, heads turned to stare at them, and the familiar feeling of overwhelming shyness overcame her.

Unconsciously, her steps slowed just slightly, and she started thinking of excuses that would let her leave early.

"Easy, baby," Storm told her softly. "It's okay."

Damn, she thought she'd hidden her reluctance.

These were his people. His SEALs. Raising her chin, she put on a brave face and made a vow to herself to do whatever it took not to embarrass the man next to her.

"That's my girl," he told her.

And even that little bit of praise made her feel better.

Storm walked them over to Rear Admiral Dag Creasy. Except he looked very different than the way she usually saw him. Instead of his uniform, he had on a pair of swimming trunks and a tank top. Jane knew he was only a few years older than her, but he was still very much in shape.

"'Bout time you made it," Dag teased Storm.

The man at her side didn't even tense. He simply shrugged. "Hey, you're the one who keeps telling me I need to relax more. So this morning, I relaxed and slept in. Can't have it both ways."

The rear admiral chuckled. "True." He turned to Jane. "Good to see you again, Jane. How are you?"

"I'm good, Sir," she said.

"None of that 'sir' shit today," he told her immediately. "It's Dag."

"Yes, Sir...er...Dag," Jane said awkwardly.

The pretty woman at his side grinned and held out her hand. "Hi. I'm Brenae, Dag's wife. It's good to meet you."

"I'm Jane," she told her.

"Sorry, I should've done the introductions," Storm said with a squeeze of the hand he was still holding. "Jane works in our building and is responsible for the mail. She does a hell of a job organizing all the shit that gets sent to us, and I don't think operations on base would run as smoothly as they do without her."

Jane blushed. "He's exaggerating," she told Brenae.

"I doubt it," the rear admiral's wife said. "I know Storm, and he doesn't compliment anyone lightly. If he said it, he believes it." Her eyes flicked down to where Storm was holding Jane's hand, and she smiled. "Welcome to the family," she said easily.

"Oh, but—"

"Thanks." Storm interrupted whatever Jane was going to say.

"I saw Rocco and the others over that way, and Wolf and his team ave commandeered the prime piece of beach real estate next to them,")ag told them. "They were all asking about you earlier. You might go and et the hellos out of the way before you get Jane a drink."

"Sounds good."

"Oh, and I know it's Saturday and all…but I wanted to tell you that JCIS called late last night. They think they know who sent the bomb."

"They do?" Storm asked. "Who?"

"Lieutenant Simon Sandburg."

Jane looked up at Storm and saw no recognition in his face. Dag bviously saw the same thing, because he kept talking.

"He was a lieutenant who was court-martialed for misappropriation f government property."

"That's right," Storm said, nodding. "I remember that case. He was 1e guy who was in charge of the heavy equipment, and he had his unit vorking jobs for the locals and was pocketing the money, right?"

"That's him. He also couldn't account for several heavy trucks when . came time to come back to the States. NCIS tracked his accounts and lagged several unidentified deposits, but he refused to tell them where he ot the money," Dag said. "He was court-martialed six months ago and is till in the area. He wasn't shy about telling anyone who would listen that 1e'd been screwed, and that the real people who should've been lisciplined were the commanders of the base."

"They were cleared, right?" Storm asked.

"Yup. Clean as a whistle. Sandburg was guilty as hell and apparently 3 just bitter he got a dishonorable discharge. He hasn't found a job since 1e was kicked out, and I'm told he spends a lot of his time at the local ›ubs drowning his sorrows. Shit thing of it all is that he's got a wife who's vorking her ass off to keep their heads above water, but it isn't enough. VCIS says they're going to lose their house in a few months."

Storm whistled. "Sounds like he's got an ax to grind."

"Yup. Anyway, I just wanted you to know. NCIS and the local cops .re going to talk to him this weekend." Dag looked at Jane. "So you won't 1ave to keep looking over your shoulder for too much longer."

"Good," Jane told him. She didn't want to admit that she hadn't eally been too worried. It was always in the back of her mind, especially ince Storm had warned her to be on the lookout, but she never seriously thought anyone would be after her. She didn't have anything to do with Sandburg being discharged, so there was no reason for him to come after her.

"I love you, Dag, but...enough. We're here to relax and have fun, not talk shop," Brenae lightly scolded.

"Sorry, sweetheart. You're right. We'll talk later," Dag told Storm.

Storm gave the rear admiral a chin lift, then he was pulling her away.

"Nice to meet you, Brenae," she called out as Storm led them toward his men.

"Same!" the other woman returned with a smile and wave. "Have fun!"

Storm didn't give her time to worry about meeting his men. One second they were walking down the beach toward them, and the next they were surrounded.

"Hey, Sir!"

"Good to see you, North!"

"You're late!"

The greetings came fast and furious, and Jane couldn't help but smile. The men seemed down-to-earth, and she loved that they didn't hesitate to give their commanding officer hell. In her experience, the more relaxed people were around their boss when they weren't at work, the better the boss.

"Yeah, yeah, yeah," Storm told his men. "No offense, but I'd rather hang out and stare at Jane than your ugly mugs."

Everyone burst out laughing. Jane knew she was blushing, but she couldn't help her huge smile.

"Everyone, this is Jane. I think most of you have seen her around the base. Jane, this is Rocco, Gumby, Ace, Bubba, Rex, and Phantom. They're a hell of a SEAL team, even if they are a little rough around the edges."

"It's good to meet you," Rocco said, holding out a hand.

Jane shook it. "You too," she told him. Then she did the same with the other five men. When it was Phantom's turn, he held her hand for a little longer than necessary. Jane felt as if he was examining her as they locked gazes. Finally, he nodded before dropping his hand. She had no idea what he'd been looking for, but hopefully he wasn't too disappointed in whatever he'd seen.

"I've heard a lot about you, Phantom," she told the extremely tall man. "All good things," she hurried to clarify.

"Then whoever you've been talking to was lying," he told her calmly.

His friends all laughed, but Jane didn't even smile.

She shook her head. "Nope. I know you've got a reputation for being extremely gruff, but anyone who did what you did…risked your own life and career to rescue someone who desperately needed a champion is someone I'm proud to know."

Jane felt Storm squeeze her hand, but she didn't take her gaze from Phantom's.

He stared at her for a moment longer before nodding and looking at Storm. "She'll do," he said, then turned and headed for a red-haired woman behind him.

"That's high praise coming from Phantom," Rocco told her. "We've all seen you around and appreciate your efficiency. I remember one time when I'd been called down to the mail room because I was expecting a very important package, and no one seemed to know where the hell it was even though the tracking showed that it had been delivered to the base. You personally took the time to track it down. It had been delivered to the wrong office, and the secretary there was new and was too busy trying to learn everything else about her job to deal with it. I appreciate you going out of your way to find it."

Jane nodded. She didn't remember the specific incident Rocco was talking about. She spent a lot of time trying to find misplaced letters and packages. "I'm glad I was able to find it for you," she told him.

Just then, a little girl ran up to Ace and hugged him around the waist. "Come play, Daddy!" she begged. Ace lifted her off her feet and turned her upside down. The girl shrieked. "You wanna play, Rani?" he asked. Then he gave Jane a smile and headed toward two other girls who looked more than ready to play with their dad. A blonde woman who Jane assumed was his wife merely shook her head at his antics.

One by one, the other men on Rocco's team told her they were glad to meet her then headed back to their wives and families. If Jane had stumbled onto the beach party on her own, she never in a hundred years would've guessed that she was looking at deadly SEALs.

"Ready to meet my other team?" Storm asked.

Jane took a deep breath. "Bring it," she mumbled.

Storm chuckled and leaned down to kiss her cheek. "For what it's worth…they liked you."

Jane rolled her eyes.

"What? They did," he insisted.

"Storm, you're their boss. They wouldn't let on if they didn't like me.

And meeting me for two seconds isn't enough for them to know if they liked me or not."

"Wrong," Storm said immediately. "These aren't men who suffer fools. I made the mistake of bringing a woman I was casually dating to one of these things years ago, and it was made more than clear that no one thought she was good enough for me."

"How?" Jane asked.

Storm shrugged. "Little things. They didn't shake her hand. Didn't engage in any kind of small talk. Talked to me like she wasn't there. They were actually pretty rude, but their point was made. So, you see, baby, they more than approve of you."

"So what are *we* doing?" she asked.

"What do you mean?" he asked, frowning.

"You said you brought a woman you were casually dating. Is that what we're doing?" She hated feeling insecure but couldn't help it.

"No," he said firmly. "We aren't casually doing anything. If we were, you wouldn't be waking up in my bed as much as you are. I can count on one hand the number of women who I've slept the whole night with."

She stared at him in disbelief. "Really?"

"Really," he confirmed. "You ready to meet Wolf and the others now?"

She nodded, feeling chastised and special at the same time.

The meeting with the second SEAL team went similarly as it had with Rocco and the others. The men were polite, and their wives were extremely friendly and open. Their kids were well mannered, and everyone seemed happy to meet her.

Afterward, Jane relaxed for the first time, happy that the introductions were over and she could sit and enjoy the day with Storm by her side.

They stayed for three hours, laughing with each other, and Jane even joined some of the wives when they took the kids for a snow cone break.

All in all, it had been an amazing day. Jane shouldn't have been surprised at how many people had known her, but she still was. She'd been working on the base a very long time, and apparently her hard work and attention to detail had made more of a difference than she'd realized.

They were on their way home, and Storm had her hand in his, as usual. He glanced at her. "You look...content."

"I am," she told him immediately.

"Everyone loved you. Not that I doubted they would."

"I enjoyed meeting everyone you work with very much. I can see ow why you work so hard to make sure you have as much information s possible before they go off on missions."

Storm nodded seriously. "They're good men. Very good men. And 'd never forgive myself if I sent them into a shit-storm and someone nded up permanently hurt or dead. You saw their wives and families oday. I never want to deprive anyone of their husband or father."

"There were other teams that weren't here today, right?" she asked.

Storm nodded. "Yeah. Wolf and his guys no longer go on active nissions. They stay here and help train the newer teams and help out luring BUD/S. But I've got two other teams that I work with who ouldn't come today. One is training, and the other guys are on temporary luty in Hawaii."

"That doesn't sound too bad," Jane said with a smile.

"Oh, Hawaii is nice, but the team they're working with takes great pleasure in flattening anyone who comes out to train with them. It's way nore humid in Hawaii than here in Southern California, and while my guys can adapt to just about anything, it takes a toll." Storm chuckled.

"You've met them?" Jane asked, extremely curious about anyone torm worked with.

"I've met their team leader, Mustang. He came to Phantom's Admiral's Mast. He was a witness and was one hundred percent upportive of him."

"Wow, he knows Phantom?" Jane asked.

"The SEAL community is tight. And Phantom and Kalee spent some ime with Mustang and his team while they were in Hawaii."

Jane nodded. She'd heard the story about how Phantom had brought Kalee to Hawaii to try to reacclimate to life after being a captive of the ebels in Timor-Leste, where he'd rescued her.

"Mustang, Midas, Aleck, Pid, Jag, and Slate are good men."

"I think you'd say that about *all* SEAL teams," Jane teased.

"Actually, I wouldn't," Storm replied seriously. "I mean, they're all technically proficient, but some teams just work better together than others. Some men click and work like a well-oiled machine."

"Yeah, I've had some employees like that."

Storm smiled over at her. "I'm glad you had a good time today. You seemed to get along well with the women."

"I did. They were all very welcoming and open. I know that's because I was with you, though."

"Nope. It's because that's just who they are," Storm told her. "And because you're easy to be around. I felt that way from the very beginning. You're calming, and when I'm around you, I feel more relaxed."

Jane wasn't sure what to say to that, so she simply smiled at him.

"You got a bit of sun today," he told her. "How do you feel about baths?"

"Love them. Why?"

"Because I thought I'd run you one when we get home. You can relax and soak while I make us something light to eat. Then I thought we could watch one of the multitude of movies I've got collecting dust on my shelf."

"I'd love that," Jane told him. As much as she enjoyed making love with him, she wasn't as young as she used to be and was tired from being in the sun all day and having to be "on" all afternoon. A quiet night vegging in front of the TV and snuggling with her man sounded idyllic. "But you don't always have to cook for me," she protested.

"I enjoy it," he told her honestly. "Cooking for myself is boring and gets old. I love spoiling you."

"Far be it from me to protest," she told him, then changed the subject. "Do you think Dag is worried about this Sandburg guy?" She'd thought about what he'd said on and off all day, and it bothered her that Dag might still be in danger.

Storm shook his head. "No. Now that NCIS has him on their radar, he won't be a threat for much longer. I'm sure by Monday things will be resolved, and we can all relax."

"Until the next person who thinks that violence will make them feel better or solve their problems," Jane muttered.

"True. But how about for tonight, and the rest of the weekend, we try not to think about work and enjoy our time together?"

"Deal," Jane said immediately.

"Go ahead and close your eyes, it'll take another half an hour or so to get through this traffic and get home."

Home. Jane liked the sound of that more than she should for the amount of time she'd been dating Storm. But she merely nodded and rested her head on the seat behind her.

Chapter Ten

When Monday morning rolled around, Storm was ninety-nine percent sure he wanted to spend the rest of his life with Jane. The weekend had been perfect. They clicked and meshed so easily it was as if they'd known each other their entire lives.

Usually by this point in a relationship, Storm was feeling antsy and couldn't wait to go back to his old routine of being alone. But he couldn't imagine spending even one day without talking to or being with Jane. He'd spent his entire life looking for her but hadn't known it until they'd met. If he believed in that sort of thing, he'd think they were meant to be together. Divine fate or reincarnated lovers. Whatever it was…he was going to do everything in his power to hold on to her and treat her so good she'd never want to leave him.

They'd made love yesterday afternoon, and it had been slow and lazy. He'd never thought he'd be in a kind of relationship where cuddling was almost as satisfying as being inside her. But he was now.

He hated having to go back to the "real world," and for the first time in his career, Storm actually looked forward to a life outside the Navy. He'd given a hell of a lot to his country and couldn't wait until he didn't have to get up at the crack of dawn to give even more, especially when he thought of waking up to Jane.

He locked his door and headed toward the parking lot with Jane at his side. He'd driven her around all weekend, and it didn't feel right to part with her now…but he was a grown-ass man, just as she was a grown-ass woman, and they both had jobs to get to.

"Are you going to have a lunch break today?" he asked.

Jane shook her head. "I don't usually have time on Mondays. The mail from Saturday is stacked up, and it's easier to skip lunch and get it out than to let it continue to pile up."

"Are you coming back here tonight?" he asked hopefully.

Jane turned to look at him. "Do you... Are we rushing this?" she asked.

"No," Storm told her immediately. "I mean, we've moved fast, but it feels right. Doesn't it?"

"It does, but the absolute last thing I want is to move things so fast that you'll regret it."

"I won't," Storm told her emphatically. "But if you want to slow things down, I'll respect that."

"You could come over to my apartment..." she said tentatively, letting her words trail off.

"Deal," Storm told her.

"I know my bed's not as big and you have a better kitchen," she told him.

"Doesn't matter. Wherever you are is where I want to be." He saw her flush.

"You're too good to me," she said.

"No such thing," Storm swore, then leaned down and kissed her briefly. "We've got to get to work or we'll be late. I'll follow you, like usual." He loved that they left for work at the same time. He would've preferred to be driving her, but they really did both need their cars just in case they needed to go off base at some point in the day. Storm was looking forward to the day she'd feel comfortable taking his Golf when she needed to run an errand, but he'd deal for now.

"Okay. Drive safe," she told him.

"You too, baby," Storm replied, squeezing her hand once more before dropping it and heading for his car. He looked back once to see Jane watching him and lifted his chin in her direction. She gave him a small wave and headed for her Camry. When she'd come over on Friday night, the parking lot had been packed, and she'd had to park a few rows over from where his car was located.

Storm arrived at his vehicle and started it. He took a minute to glance at his email once more before putting his car in gear and backing out. He pulled around to where Jane had been and saw that she was already pulling out of the parking lot.

It was unusual for her not to wait for him to pull up behind her, but e didn't think much about it. They were running a bit late, probably because he'd been reluctant to get out of bed and had spent an extra ten minutes simply holding her against him that morning after the alarm had gone off. She was probably just anxious to get to work and not to be late.

Storm headed out of the parking lot and caught up to Jane fairly quickly. Then he frowned—something seemed out of place.

It took him a moment to figure out what it was, and when he did, the hair on the back of his neck stood on end.

There was someone in the car with Jane. Sitting in the front seat next to her. He couldn't imagine who she could've met and agreed to give a ride to in the thirty seconds or so when she'd been out of his sight.

When they stopped at a light, Jane didn't look in her rearview window and wave at him, like she often did.

Something was wrong. He knew it in his gut.

And Storm knew better than to ignore his gut. It had saved his life more than once when he'd been a SEAL. He hadn't felt this way in a very long time, but he'd never forget or dismiss the feeling.

Picking up his phone, he dialed a number he'd memorized a long time ago…just in case. The Navy police.

* * * *

Jane held on to her steering wheel and stared straight ahead, too terrified to do anything that would set off the woman sitting next to her. One second she'd been smiling and relaxed, remembering how sweet Storm had been that morning, and the next, a woman had opened her passenger-side door and shoved a knife against her side and told her to drive.

She would've bailed out of the car there and then because she knew better than to let a carjacker take her someplace where it would be easier to kill her and dump her dead body, except the woman said in a low voice, "This box in my lap has a bomb in it. If you don't do exactly what I say, we're both going to be blown to itty-bitty pieces, and no one will ever find all our parts."

Somehow, Jane knew she wasn't lying. So she put her car in gear and drove.

"I'm Jane. What's your name?" she asked, thinking if they were on a first-name basis, maybe she'd be less likely to kill her.

"Not that it matters, since we'll both be dead if you don't do exactly as I say, but it's Carlin. I saw you on TV," the woman said nonchalantly as Jane drove toward the naval base. "I bet that CS gas hurt, didn't it?"

Carlin seemed calm enough at the moment, but Jane couldn't help glancing down at the box in her lap. It looked so…ordinary. But if she'd been able to rig a tear gas bomb, Jane had no doubt she'd be able to make something more deadly.

Her palms were sweaty on the steering wheel, and she wanted nothing more than to send some sort of signal to Storm, who she knew was behind her, but she was scared the woman in the seat next to her would catch on and do something drastic. So she decided to just try to stay calm and do whatever was asked of her…at least for the time being.

"Yeah, it sucked," Jane said honestly.

Carlin shrugged. "It wasn't meant for you," she somewhat apologized. "Rear Admiral Creasy was the one who was supposed to open it."

"Why?" Jane asked simply.

"Because he's an asshole!" she said. "He didn't even think twice about kicking my husband out of the Navy. Simon worked his ass off, and he was helping those pathetic locals overseas. He'd never steal money from *anyone*. His commanders had everything all wrong, and when he tried to explain, they wouldn't even listen! Kicked him out without breaking a sweat. Ruined his life—*and* mine."

Jane blinked in surprise. She remembered Dag and Storm talking about Lieutenant Simon Sandburg. At the time, they'd thought the person who'd sent the bomb was him, but evidence was currently suggesting otherwise.

"I'm sorry," Jane said, not sure what to say to seem both sympathetic and empathetic at the same time. "Sounds like you've had a hard time of it lately."

"Damn straight I have," Carlin said. "I've worked like a dog to keep things going, all the while trying to encourage Simon to find another job, to do *something*. But instead he spends all his time—and our spare money—at the bar, drowning his sorrows. I told him we could hire a lawyer, prove that he was innocent, and the money was given to him by people who were so thankful someone was helping them, but he refuses."

Jane wanted to roll her eyes. Could she really be that stupid?

"I mean, nothing's wrong with a military member getting thank-you gifts. That asshole Creasy wouldn't even listen to him during his court-martial. The entire thing took less than ten minutes. *Ten minutes*, and our ves were ruined. Fucking asshole! He'll regret kicking Simon out. I'll nake sure of it."

"What's your plan?" Jane asked, both needing to know the answer nd dreading it at the same time.

"Well, I was going to wait until the scrutiny died down, then strike vhen Creasy least expected it, but after those NCIS guys came to our lace this weekend and grilled Simon, I had to move my timetable. Those ssholes aren't going to be happy until they completely demoralize my usband. I have to get on base," Carlin told her. "I couldn't send the kind f bomb I wanted last time. I knew it would get jostled too much and the xplosive would be set off before I wanted it to. I thought I'd perfected he CS bomb to go off only when the box was opened, but apparently I vas wrong."

Yeah, apparently she was. "Then what?" Jane asked.

"I can't get on base by myself because my military ID was onfiscated when my husband was court-martialed. So I need *you* to get ne on. You'll show your ID at the gate, and I'll give them the fake lriver's license I've obtained. It'll go nice and smooth when you vouch or me. If you do that, you'll be home free. So be a good girl and don't do nything stupid," Carlin said in a hard tone. "I won't hesitate to set this ucking bomb off. I'll kill as many people as I can in the process."

Jane looked in the rearview mirror and saw Storm's car behind her. She couldn't think of any way to warn him about what was happening and vho was sitting next to her without setting Carlin off. "What about Simon?" she asked.

"What about him?" Carlin asked.

"What's he going to think about all this?"

"Once he hears what I've done, the lengths I've gone to in order to venge him, he'll be proud of me. We'll leave this fucking state, get new obs somewhere else, and live happily ever after. He just needs to put this pehind him. And making sure Creasy isn't around to make anyone else's ife miserable is just the way to do it."

Jane swallowed hard in disbelief. Did the woman really think she could deliver a bomb, kill a rear admiral, sneak off base, and live happily ever after? That her man would approve of such a thing and snap out of the funk he was in?

And what about her? Had she even thought about what a loose end Jane would be?

Carlin was sitting there telling her all her plans. She had to know Jane would go to the authorities as soon as she got out of the car.

Knowing she was in deep shit, and it was likely Carlin had some other plan for her, Jane did her best to stay calm. She couldn't panic. Had to think about what to do and be ready to get the hell out of this car at a moment's notice.

Jane thought about causing a car wreck, but that might set off the bomb in Carlin's lap. The last thing she wanted was to involve anyone else in this woman's evil plan. She didn't want to be responsible for someone losing their life.

"Why me?" Jane asked softly.

Carlin shrugged. "When I saw you on TV, I actually felt bad that you were caught in the middle of my revenge plan. You're just a lowly mailman. I tracked you down, thinking I'd apologize somehow...but then I saw you with *him*."

"Who? Creasy?" Jane asked, confused.

"No. His friend. I don't know his name, nor do I care. I followed you, realized you were fucking him. But I knew you drove separately to work. It was easy enough to hide out by your car and surprise you. Since you're sleeping with the enemy, there's no reason for me to feel sorry for you," Carlin said matter-of-factly.

Jane's head spun. "Storm isn't the enemy," she blurted, hating to hear anyone talk bad about him.

"He is!" Carlin insisted. "He hangs out with Creasy. Probably has kicked out his share of decent, hard-working sailors too. They're *all* assholes—and if you're sleeping with him, you're a bitch. So it doesn't matter if you die. In fact, since you know all about what I'm going to do, it's inevitable."

Carlin talked about killing her so nonchalantly, so easily, that Jane was shocked. And it was hard to surprise her after everything that had happened with her marriage, her daughter's troubled teenage years, and after working on the military base for so long.

"Don't try to be a hero," Carlin told her, pressing the knife she hadn't taken away from her side a bit harder into her flesh.

Jane inhaled sharply as the tip of the blade sliced through her shirt and nicked her skin. "I'm not. I won't," she said immediately, doing her best to pull her body away from the knife. But her small Camry didn't have that much room between the passenger's and driver's seats. It was a detail she loved when Storm was in the car with her. She definitely didn't like it now.

They drove toward the base in silence, and when they began to get close, Jane's heart rate accelerated, and she could feel adrenaline coursing through her veins. The best time to get away was when she had to stop at the gate. When the naval officer asked for her ID. She definitely didn't want him to get hurt, but she didn't want Creasy to die either. Or herself.

"Be cool," Carlin warned as they approached the gate to the base. Don't do anything stupid, or *kablooey*! You'll never fuck that asshole you're with again."

A drop of sweat fell down the side of Jane's face, and she knew Carlin wasn't kidding. She was insane, obviously, and if she was willing to die in order to get revenge on Rear Admiral Creasy, she wouldn't have any problem taking down anyone who stood in her way.

Looking in the rearview mirror once more, she saw that Storm had pulled up so close to her as she inched forward in the short line at the gate she couldn't even see his headlights.

Did that mean he knew something was wrong? That he had a plan?

Jane hoped with all her heart that was the case, even as she also hoped he was oblivious. The latter would mean he was safe. The former could get them all killed…

But it might just save them too.

Shit.

"IDs please," the junior-grade lieutenant said as Jane pulled up in front of the small guardhouse.

She turned to look at Carlin. She had a bright smile on her face and the knife she'd held to Jane's side was nowhere to be seen. But that damn box in her lap seemed to be even bigger than it had been earlier. That wasn't the case, of course, but Jane couldn't help but sense the danger lurking inside it.

She slowly reached for her purse to pull out her ID and saw Carlin give her an impatient look. Jane wanted to say something to the young officer. To give him some clue as to the danger they were all in, but she also didn't want to risk his life…or her own.

She grabbed the ID that allowed her access to the base and took the fake ID Carlin handed to her as well. She handed both to the officer, opening her eyes really wide, hoping against hope he'd get the hint.

Without hesitation, the man turned away from her and took the IDs into the guardhouse, as was protocol. Jane knew he'd scan them both, then if nothing seemed awry, he'd hand them back, and they'd be on their way.

Time ticked by extremely slowly. Every second seemed like an eternity. Jane glanced around without turning her head, and to her, i seemed as if there were more people hanging around the gate to the base than normal. The sky was just beginning to lighten with the rise of the sun, and she could see naval police personnel around almost every corner It made her feel hopeful, but scared shitless at the same time. More people meant more casualties if something went wrong.

After a moment, the young officer turned to her. "There's an issue with your ID, Ms. Hamilton. If you can please step out of the car."

For just a second, Jane's hopes rose. She undid her seat belt and reached for the handle of her door. She had just opened it a bit when Carlin moved.

The knife was pressed against her skin again, but this time it was a her throat.

"Step back," Carlin ordered the lieutenant. "She's not going anywhere. You're going to open the damn gate and let us through otherwise I'll gut her like a pig and set off this bomb in my lap. You have ten fucking seconds to get it done. Starting *now*."

The officer's eyes opened wide, but his eyes flicked to something behind Carlin. Without moving her head, Jane saw three naval police officers, their pistols pointed right at Carlin, out of the corner of her eye.

"Put the knife down, *now!*" one of them shouted.

Within seconds, the car was surrounded by more police officers than Jane had seen in one place since she'd started working on the base. She hadn't been around the parking lot when Phantom and his girlfriend had been attacked, but she imagined it probably looked a lot like the area around her car right now.

"Get back!" Carlin shouted a little desperately. "I've got a bomb and I'll fucking set it off! I will! Don't mess with me!"

"Just relax," one of the police officers said. "We'll figure this out, and no one will get hurt."

"But I *want* people to get hurt," Carlin screamed. "Just like my husband and I were! Get Rear Admiral Creasy here. *Right now!*"

Jane shook violently in her seat. The car was surrounded by shore patrol—SPs—or masters-at-arms…whatever the naval police were called. She couldn't remember if they were SPs when they were on a ship and masters-at-arms when they were on base, or vice versa, or both.

She *did* know her mind was going in a million different directions, and she forced herself to concentrate. It didn't matter what they were

alled. Police were police, and she prayed they'd figure out a way to get
veryone out of this in one piece. Literally.

Jane sat as still as she could, hoping against hope Carlin would
omehow forget about her sitting there, what with all the commotion
oing on around them…when she felt something brush against her left
and.

When she'd opened her door, and after Carlin had shoved the knife
ito her neck, Jane had let her hand dangle limply against her side.

But now someone was holding it. Tightly.

She couldn't look down to confirm who it was, but she'd recognize
ie feel of the callused fingers anywhere. In her panic, she'd forgotten
torm was even behind her. But he'd obviously gotten out of his car and
vas now at her side. She prayed Carlin couldn't see him.

Having him there terrified her—but it also made her more
letermined than ever to do what she could to make sure this ended
vithout her, or Storm, in tiny bits all over the asphalt.

She squeezed his hand back as hard as she could, and the way he
ightened his hold made her sigh in relief. Storm was there. He'd help her.
he just had to be ready for whatever he had in mind. And she had no
loubt he had a plan.

Once a SEAL, always a SEAL.

* * * *

Storm watched with his heart in his throat as Jane pulled up to the
;uardhouse at the entrance to the naval base. After Storm's call to the
>olice to inform them to be on the lookout for Jane's car, the junior-grade
>fficer was more than aware that something was hinky. He'd been
nstructed to act normal, however, and to get Jane out of the car as
inobtrusively as possible.

As her car stopped, Storm pulled up to it as closely as he could get
ind slipped out of the driver's seat. He immediately got down on his belly
ind crawled toward Jane's door. The second she stepped out, he would be
here to grab her and get her to safety. Everyone else could deal with
vhoever was sitting next to her.

The hair on the back of his neck hadn't gone down. He knew
;omething was very wrong, and his only objective was to get Jane clear of
t. He regretted not insisting they drive together, and in the future, he'd be
;ure to do a better job of keeping her safe.

But his plans went down the drain when the woman sitting next to her refused to let Jane exit the vehicle. Storm's mind spun. He heard her say she had a bomb, and while he couldn't see either of them, he also heard her say something about gutting Jane.

Looking up through the crack of her door—which thankfully Jane hadn't shut—Storm could see how white she was. She was sitting stiff in her seat, and her left arm was motionless at her side.

Without thought, as everyone yelled for the unknown woman to stand down, to give herself up, Storm reached for Jane's hand.

Her fingers were ice cold, and he knew it was because of shock setting in. He thought she might panic when he took hold of her, but he should've known better. The second his fingers closed around her own, she relaxed. Not completely, but enough that he was assured she knew who was touching her.

And when she squeezed his fingers back, determination rose up within him once more.

He wasn't going to lose her. No fucking way. He had no idea if the woman sitting next to her had a real bomb or not, but he wasn't going to take any chances.

By some miracle, Storm was still undetected, and he crouched down even lower. He didn't want the other woman to catch a glimpse of him in the side mirror. One wrong move and they could all be blown up. He hadn't gone forty-seven years without having found the one person meant to be his only to lose her now.

No. Just no.

The longer Storm crouched by the car and listened to the woman rant on and on and demand the officers bring Creasy out, the more determined he became. A plan formed in his mind, and he turned his head to look around him. His position wasn't ideal. Jane's car was close to the guard shack, which didn't leave them much room. But she'd pulled up far enough that the opening to the shack would be behind the door just far enough when it was opened.

Nodding to himself, Storm looked around, trying to see who else was there. He saw a lot of young SPs and older officers, as well—but not who he needed to see.

He'd called Rocco right after he'd contacted the naval police, but he knew it would take time for him to arrive. And he'd surely called his team. Soon, his SEALs would arrive.

Hurry up, guys. I need you, Storm thought to himself. He knew the SPs would stall the woman as long as they could, but she was obviously unstable, and there was no telling how much time they had before she lost her patience and either stabbed Jane or blew them all up.

* * * *

"Where is he?" Carlin yelled impatiently. "You aren't *listening* to me! I'll do it, I've got nothing to lose! Bring Creasy here so I can talk to him. That's all I want!"

"We're working on it," the man who'd been attempting to negotiate with Carlin replied.

"Work on it faster!" she screeched. "If you think I'm fucking around, I'm not. I've already set off one bomb on this base, and I'll do it again! But this time it'll do some fucking damage! If you don't want to be responsible for the deaths of everyone within hearing distance, you'll get him here now!"

Jane tuned out Carlin and did her best to come up with a plan. She could slam her foot on the gas and do whatever she could to get the car away from the gate and all the people before Carlin set off the bomb. But there was no guarantee she could get the car into gear and get out of the way before the bomb exploded. She could try to wrestle the knife and box away from Carlin, but again, maybe the slightest movement would set off the damn thing and everyone would get killed anyway. She could wait for the negotiators to do their job, but it wasn't looking like Carlin was going to back down. Jane didn't know if seeing and talking to Creasy would help or make the situation worse.

Glancing in the rearview mirror, Jane saw a large Chevy pickup careen around the other vehicles that had been evacuated in the line behind her. She recognized it. Gumby, one of Storm's men, owned one like it. She'd seen it at the beach party…was that just two days ago?

Hope welled up inside her, and for the second time—the first being when she realized Storm was holding her hand—she thought she might just get out of this alive. She didn't know how, but if anyone could figure it out, it was Storm and his team.

"I'm losing patience!" Carlin screamed, waving the knife that had been at Jane's throat. She jabbed it uselessly out the window toward the negotiator who was standing at least twenty feet from the car. "Get. Me. Creasy! He needs to know that his actions have consequences! If he didn't unfairly court-martial my husband, this wouldn't be happening!"

The sun was just beginning to peek above the horizon now, and as it so happened, the gate was facing east. Jane winced, knowing the sun would blind her as it rose. In ten minutes it wouldn't be a nuisance, but in the few minutes it took to climb high enough in the sky, it would make it impossible to see anything going on in front of the vehicle.

"*Fuck*," Carlin swore from next to her. "This has all gone to shit!"

The sun suddenly rose high enough in the sky to send its blinding rays right into the eyes of Jane and the agitated woman next to her.

Then Jane felt Storm squeeze her hand, hard.

She tensed and held her breath. This was it. Whatever Storm had planned was about to happen. She hoped like hell if it didn't work, and that damn bomb went off, that her death would be fast. She'd never been afraid of dying, but she wasn't a fan of pain.

Feeling ashamed of the direction her thoughts had wandered, Jane wasn't prepared when her car door slammed open, Storm yanked her arm hard enough to almost pull it from its socket, and she went flying through the air.

* * * *

Storm was relieved when Gumby, Rocco, and Bubba jumped out of Gumby's Silverado and stealthily made their way to the other side of the guard shack. The woman—who he now knew was Lieutenant Simon Sandburg's wife because of all her screaming—was concentrating on what was going on to her right with the police and the negotiator. She clearly assumed with the guardhouse so close to her left, there would be no danger there.

She'd thought wrong. She had no clue that some of the most deadly men in the world were about to end this standoff once and for all.

Dag had been advised to stay out of sight, but Storm knew he was there somewhere. The second he heard there was a situation at the gate, he would've wanted to be there, even if his presence *wasn't* being demanded. Storm hadn't seen him, but he had no doubt he was watching and waiting for just the right time to make his presence known.

And if he let Carlin Sandburg see him, Storm knew she'd blow that bomb in her lap, if only in the vague hope that it would kill him too.

Turning his attention to his SEALs, Storm saw that Bubba was holding his Navy-issued sniper rifle. He was the best shot on the team, and Storm had never been so thankful to see anyone in his entire life. He

vasn't a fan of killing anyone, but he knew Bubba would be able to
ncapacitate Carlin without killing her, hopefully bringing this standoff to
n end safely.

He gestured to the front of the vehicle with his head, knowing the
un's position would temporarily blind both Jane and Carlin. He'd been in
ine often enough to know what a pain in the ass the sunrise was while
oming onto base at this time. They'd lucked out, and any moment now,
ie and the other SEALs could use that to their advantage.

Understanding, his men nodded. He pointed to where his hand was
idden by the door, hoping they'd figure out that he had hold of Jane. He
hen spun his free hand in circles and pointed in the direction in which he
olanned on extricating Jane from the vehicle.

Rocco nodded and said something to his teammates. Then Bubba
ind Gumby headed for positions directly in front of the car behind a
oolice vehicle that had parked there to prevent Jane from getting onto the
oase, and Rocco disappeared around the edge of the guard shack.

Storm held his breath. There was no guarantee this would work. If
Carlin was as good of an engineer as reports had indicated, they could all
oe in deep shit. The tear gas bomb she'd built had been good, so he had
io doubt that the box in her lap was legit and could kill them all, like she
claimed.

Determination welled up within Storm once again. *No one* fucked
with his Jane.

Time seemed to slow down as he waited for the sun to get to the
oerfect point in the sky. Carlin's tone got more and more agitated, and for
a second, Storm thought they weren't going to make it. That she'd get
impatient and decide she was done waiting for Creasy to show up and
detonate the bomb.

One second the air was filled with tense anticipation, and the next,
he first rays of the sun burst above the horizon as if a beacon from God,
pointing His finger at Carlin in condemnation.

It was a fanciful thought, and Storm didn't have time to dwell on it.
He knew he and his team had only seconds to act. That Carlin would
realize her front side was vulnerable and surely someone would make a
move to stop her deadly plans.

Looking up at Bubba, who he could see was lifting the rifle from
about thirty yards in front of Jane's vehicle, Storm held his breath.

He squeezed Jane's hand hard, trying to warn her that the shit was
about to hit the fan. He felt her tense—and then he moved.

Storm wrenched the car door open and pulled Jane toward him with all his strength.

She practically flew out of the seat and into his arms. He threw them both backward toward the open door of the guard shack as fast as he could. Storm needed to put as much distance between them and that bomb as possible.

He was counting on the suddenness of his movements to take Carlin off guard. That it would take her a moment to realize what was happening, that her hostage was escaping, before she could detonate the bomb in her lap. He hoped she would just give up—but he'd seen his share of both desperate and crazy people in his life, and he knew she wouldn't go down easily.

Unfortunately for him and Jane, he was right. He heard Carlin scream a frustrated and anguished "no!" the moment Jane cleared the car...

A shot sounded from somewhere around them...

And then the world exploded.

Maybe not the world, but the car Jane had been sitting in seconds earlier.

Storm had managed to get them both through the guard shack and out the other side before the bomb went off, and he rolled until Jane was under him. He would've run with her, but didn't want to do anything that would leave her vulnerable. Staying put wasn't exactly safe, but was better than shrapnel tearing through her body as they ran. He covered her body with his own, closed his eyes, and prayed harder than he'd ever prayed in his life. The dubious protection of the guard shack wasn't going to be enough to keep them completely safe, but he just hoped it would save their lives.

The noise was loud, deafening. Storm felt pain slam into his back as the bulletproof windows in the guard shack exploded, no match for the force of the bomb.

"Storm!" Jane cried from under him, but he didn't budge. He held her tighter as debris rained down on them from what seemed like every direction. Despite his ears ringing and his back throbbing in pain, Storm refused to move, even when he thought the worst was past. He wasn't going to take a chance that Carlin had survived and would come after Jane.

"Storm..." Jane called out again.

She sounded stressed, and Storm knew he had to check to make sure she hadn't been hurt. That she wasn't bleeding out or anything and eeded medical assistance. He lifted his head a fraction of an inch and felt omething fall off him. It seemed as if they were mostly buried under hat was left of the guard shack. While it had collapsed on them, it had lso protected them from the worst of the blast.

Storm's back and legs throbbed, but he was alive. Jane was alive.

He looked into her eyes and saw that her pupils were so dilated, he lmost couldn't see the beautiful brown irises he'd fallen head over heels a love with.

"Storm?" she asked again.

Her hand was still in his, and he was holding it tightly between them. Are you okay?" he croaked.

Her eyes immediately filled with tears, and just as he began to panic, he nodded. "Thanks to you, yes."

"Fuck," he said under his breath, the relief almost a palpable thing. "I ove you," he blurted, not even caring that now probably wasn't the time or place for such a declaration. "The second I saw someone in your car with you, I knew something was wrong. I'm not letting you go," he owed. "You might not love me yet, but you will. I'll do whatever it akes."

"I do," she told him, tears spilling over the sides of her eyes and lown her temples to be absorbed into her dusty hair. "I think I've loved ou forever."

That was all Storm needed to hear. His lips came down on hers, and ne kissed her as if she was the most precious thing in his life...because he was. "I thought I'd lost you," he mumbled desperately.

"I knew you'd somehow get me out of there," she told him.

Storm hadn't been so sure, but he didn't contradict her.

"Sir?" they heard someone call from above them. "Get this fucking lebris off them!"

Storm groaned as a piece of wood was removed from his back.

"Are you all right?" Jane asked worriedly.

He opened his mouth to say he was fine, that he'd been hurt much worse on some of his SEAL missions, but instead, he closed his eyes and lid his best not to pass out when a board shifted across his legs and omething sharp dug into his calf.

"Stop!" Jane yelled, making Storm wince since she'd yelled forcefully, oractically in his ear. "Storm's hurt! Be fucking careful!"

He couldn't help but chuckle at that. He didn't care how many nails had to be pulled out of his back and legs. Jane was safe, and that was all he cared about.

"Hey, Sir," Rocco said in an obnoxiously cheerful voice. "You wan to continue to lay there smooching on your woman, or do you think you might want to get up and get out of here?"

"Fuck off, sailor," Storm told him, doing his best not to wince when someone took hold of his arm to help him stand.

He accepted Gumby and Bubba's assistance, then immediately turned to help Jane. When they were both upright, and Jane was against his side snuggled into him, he looked around in disbelief.

They looked like they were standing in the middle of a war zone Both his and Jane's cars were totaled. The guard shack was rubble, but i had done exactly what he'd hoped: blocked the worst of the blast and gave them just enough protection to withstand the shock wave from the bomb.

When he saw what was left of the woman who'd been sitting next to Jane—basically a few body parts here and there—he turned to block Jane's view.

"Come on," Bubba said quietly. "Let's get you to the medics."

Storm had no idea how bad his injuries were, but if his SEALs were encouraging him to go straight to the medics, they were bad enough. But Storm was upright and able to walk, even if each step made pain shoot through his body.

"You okay, Jane?" Rocco asked in a more serious tone.

"I'm good," she told him. "Storm protected me."

Rocco nodded as if that was the most normal thing he'd heard that morning. "For what it's worth, I think his injuries look worse than they are. Whatever you do, don't coddle the man. He'll get soft, then take it out on us."

Jane's lips twitched, but she didn't smile. It was too soon. Storm knew she'd have some more bad times after this. Who wouldn't? He didn't know what had happened in her car or what was said...but he would. Jane would tell him everything. Then he'd do whatever it took to make her feel safe and grounded again. Just as he knew she'd do what she could to reassure *him* that she was fine.

Leaning over, Storm kissed her temple as they walked. The movement made whatever was sticking out of his shoulder shift, and he huffed out a painful breath. But he knew whatever happened from this moment forward, he'd get through it. Jane loved him, and he loved her. Nothing else mattered.

Epilogue

Jane sat with her back straight and her hands clasped in her lap as she faced the highest-ranking officials on the base. She was there to tell her side of what had happened a month ago with Carlin Sandburg. The investigation was finally being wrapped up, after many interviews with various people.

Rear Admiral Creasy was there, along with several other officers. There was even a vice admiral in attendance who'd flown in to hear the official findings of the investigation.

Jane learned that Bubba had shot at Carlin to try to stop her so she wouldn't be able to set off the bomb, but he'd been a fraction of a second too late. She'd already detonated the explosive in her lap.

The deceased Navy spouse hadn't lied about what was in the box. But fortunately, while it had been a deadly blast, it hadn't been powerful enough to take out the police and other innocent people standing nearby.

If Jane had been sitting next to her, though, she certainly would've been blown to pieces like Carlin had.

Storm had suffered from a bruised kidney, and he had a few nails embedded in his legs and his lower back and one shoulder, but miraculously, he wasn't hurt any worse than that. Jane had felt guilty that he'd gotten hurt protecting her, but Storm had made it more than clear he'd do exactly the same thing again in a heartbeat, and he had no regrets at all at being the one hurt instead of her.

Former Lieutenant Sandburg had been thoroughly investigated and interviewed by NCIS, and they'd determined that he'd had no involvement or knowledge of his wife's plans. He also hadn't known she'd been responsible for the CS gas bomb and that she'd had plans to assassinate the rear admiral.

He wasn't at the final hearing today because he'd moved out of California to hopefully get his shit together and to separate himself from what his wife had done.

"Can you tell us in your own words what happened that morning?" the lead investigator from the NCIS asked.

Jane nodded. She'd already told her story over and over again to others. At first it had been hard, and she'd had nightmares. But over the last month, with each retelling, the hold Carlin had over her nightmares had lessened. Jane no longer woke up with a scream, thinking the bomb had gone off when she was still in the car. She no longer had nightmares where Storm was blown to pieces as he tried to save her. She was getting on with her life, and it had a hell of a lot to do with the man sitting next to her.

She felt a hand land on her thigh and squeeze softly. Glancing over at Storm, she saw him give her an almost undetectable little chin lift, and it made her feel stronger. With him by her side, she could do anything.

So she told the story of when she'd been hit by the tear gas bomb Carlin had sent, and everything she could remember between the time the woman had gotten in her car to when Storm had pulled her out of the vehicle to the dubious safety of the other side of the guard shack at the base's gate.

She answered all their questions honestly.

No, she hadn't met Carlin Sandburg before that morning.

No, she hadn't been aware that Dag had court-martialed her husband, Simon Sandburg.

Yes, she'd been afraid for her life.

No, she hadn't known what Storm had planned to do.

No, she didn't hear the shot Bubba had taken.

Jane patiently answered each and every question thrown at her, and didn't even feel irritation that some were asked twice. She understood that something of this magnitude happening at the entrance to the base was a huge deal. Every security measure was being examined with a fine-tooth comb, and they were even rethinking the way cars were funneled through the gate as a result of what had happened.

And then, finally, the questions stopped.

"Rear Admiral," the lead investigator said, "we've concluded that the ecision you made to court-martial Lieutenant Sandburg was appropriate nd not excessive. Ms. Hamilton, you are to be commended for staying alm in a less-than-ideal situation. Admiral North, your actions, along with hose of your men, were brave and surely kept more people from being ijured. Thank you all for your assistance in the investigation, and if you ave any questions about these proceedings or the outcome, you're more han welcome to discuss it with me and my team. The full written report ill be available to those who have the proper security clearance. Have a ood day."

And just like that, it was over.

Storm didn't wait around. He immediately stood, took her hand, and eaded for the door.

"North?" the vice admiral called out, and Jane wanted to laugh at the ook of impatience that crossed her man's face. He obviously wanted to gnore the hailing but knew it wasn't a good idea to dismiss someone with rank as high as the vice admiral's.

He turned. "Yes, Sir?"

The other man was grinning, as if he knew how impatient Storm was o get the hell out of there. "I'm glad you're all right. I see great things in our future as a naval officer."

Storm nodded respectfully. "Thank you. I'm glad I'm all right too, ut more importantly, Jane is okay. I didn't do what I did for accolades, or or anyone else standing around that car. I did it for Jane, and Jane alone. And as far as my career goes, I appreciate the kudos, but I wouldn't count n me being around forever."

He turned to glance at Jane, and she almost melted at the look in his yes. It was a look of love and devotion she'd only fantasized about late at ight in her dreams. And it was aimed at her. Plain Jane Hamilton. It was lmost unreal.

Storm turned his attention back to the vice admiral. "I love the Navy. 'm proud to have served my country, and I wouldn't change a moment of my career. But I've learned what's important. I'm looking forward to pending my retirement with Jane at my side and seeing what the world as to offer…as a tourist this time, and not a SEAL."

The vice admiral nodded. "You're a lucky man."

"Yes, I am," Storm agreed. He saluted the admiral, who returned the gesture, and then Storm was pulling her out of the room once more.

"In a hurry?" Jane asked in bewilderment.

"Yup," Storm said but didn't elaborate.

"Want to tell me why?"

He pulled her through the door and into the parking lot toward her brand-new XC90. It was a high-end SUV comparable to a Toyota Highlander. Jane had tried to protest, insisting it was too expensive, too new, too fancy, but he was having none of it.

She'd continued to explain why she didn't need it until he'd turned to her right there in the middle of the dealership, took her face in his hands and told her in a tone of voice she'd never heard from him before, "I need you to be safe. And while I might not be able to be by your side every second of the day, I *can* get you the safest vehicle I can find. One that, with a touch of your thumb, lets you silently call for help with their advanced security features."

How could she continue to say no when he put it like that? So she'd given in and allowed him to get the car for her.

He'd purchased his own new vehicle too. A Hummer. It was over the top, but Storm didn't care. He'd said that if she ever got into a situation like she'd been in again, he'd just run over anyone who dared to hurt her and carry her off like a Viking of old.

It was ridiculous, but since he mostly drove her Camry and hadn't really left her side except for during the workday, it didn't bother her much.

"You'll see," Storm told her in response to her question about why he was in such a hurry.

Jane wanted to roll her eyes, but secretly she loved Storm's surprises. He was generous, and with every day that passed, she loved him more and more. It was almost scary how much he'd come to mean to her in such a short time, but she was learning to embrace each moment, and life with Storm was beautiful in a way hers had never been before.

He stood on the passenger side of her SUV and waited until she was buckled in safely, then right before he shut the door, she watched him flick the lock mechanism. She'd called him out the first time he'd done that, but when he'd explained that never again was someone going to slip into the car when she wasn't aware, she'd shut up about it.

Storm drove them toward his townhouse, and they made small talk. Jane was relieved the whole issue with Carlin and the bombs was over and done with. Dag and Brenae were safe, as were everyone else. There was no guarantee someone in the future wouldn't take offense to something a superior officer did, but she hoped it wouldn't happen while she was still working. Twice had been more than enough.

Storm pulled into the parking spot he'd arranged for her to have permanently at his complex, and she waited until he came around to her side of the car. That was another change in their routine. She didn't need him to help her out of a vehicle, but she knew for his peace of mind, he needed to do it. And it wasn't exactly a hardship to have him hold her hand as soon as she exited the car.

He led her up to his door and inside.

"So, what's my surprise?" she asked impatiently.

Storm held up a finger. "Hang on just a bit longer," he told her. "I'll be right back." Then he headed for the front door they'd just come through.

Jane was confused. They'd just gotten home. "But—"

"Wait," he interrupted, then closed the door behind him.

All Jane could do was laugh. She had no idea what he was doing, but he'd never let her down with one of his surprises yet. Once it had been matching T-shirts he'd ordered online for them that said, "Andy and Red's Boat Rentals, Zihuatanejo, Mexico." She'd laughed and knew she'd treasure the shirt forever, simply because it was from their favorite movie.

Another day, he'd taken her out to eat, and Rocco, his teammates, and their wives had all joined them. It was crowded and noisy, but she'd never had a better time getting to know the men and women who meant so much to her man. Yet another time, he'd made her dinner, drawn her a bath, then joined her in it. They hadn't had sex, but being intimate with him was more of a gift than he'd ever know. She'd almost lost that, and knowing he loved her and enjoyed simply cuddling with her was beautiful.

So she had no idea what was up Storm's sleeve now, but she knew it would be something fantastic.

Just when she was getting a little anxious, she heard the front door open once more. Standing up from the couch where she'd been waiting, Jane turned—and her mouth opened in shock when her daughter entered the room ahead of Storm.

"Rose?"

"Mom…" her daughter said. Then she raced across the room and was in her arms.

Jane blinked in surprise at the display of affection. She couldn't remember the last time Rose had initiated any kind of touch with her. Probably when she was about ten, before she'd turned so bitter.

"Are you really okay?" Rose asked quietly into Jane's shoulder.

Taking a deep breath and closing her eyes, Jane did her best to memorize this moment. It had been a very long time since Rose had cared about anything other than herself, or when and where she was going to score her next hit.

Jane opened her eyes and pulled back to look at her daughter. "I'm okay. What's brought this on?"

"I didn't know how serious it was!" Rose said. "When you called a few weeks ago, you said a woman was mad at a guy from work and tried to use you to get to him. I had no idea she'd tried to *blow you up!*"

Jane looked over her shoulder and briefly met Storm's gaze. He was leaning against the wall, watching them closely. She knew without a doubt that if Rose had done or said anything hurtful, he would've marched her ass right out of his house. Yes, he'd brought her there, but he wouldn't hesitate to kick her out as well. Jane knew that as well as she knew her own name.

He hadn't been happy hearing all the stories Jane had told him about her daughter...but that hadn't kept him from doing what he knew might make Jane happy. Namely, trying to fix her relationship with Rose.

"I'm fine," Jane reassured her daughter once more. "Storm was there, and he made sure of it."

Rose turned to him then. "Thank you," she said. "I know I thanked you over the phone when you called, but seriously...I mean it."

"Your mom means the world to me, so you're welcome. I'd do *anything* to make her happy and keep her safe."

Jane could hear the warning in his words, and apparently, so could Rose.

"I've done lots of things in my life that I've regretted," she said. "But I'm trying to change. Be a better person."

Storm nodded once.

"Can you stay for dinner?" Jane asked.

"If you want me to," Rose said tentatively.

"Of course I do," Jane answered.

"Are you cooking?" Rose teased. "Because if so, maybe I'll reconsider."

Jane chuckled. "Nope. You're safe. Storm's the cook in this house."

Rose looked over at him. "Maybe I can get some lessons?"

"Of course," Storm said immediately, then pushed off the wall to head for the kitchen.

"Hasn't Robert taught you some things?" Jane asked.

Rose shrugged. "I left him. I'd had enough of his abuse." She looked at Jane then. "I'm trying, Mom. I know I was awful to you, and to everyone around me. I took my hurt at Dad leaving out on you and did things I'm not proud of. I'm going to Narcotics Anonymous meetings every week now. Trying to get my shit together. I want to be someone you're proud of instead of the daughter you're ashamed of."

Jane reached for her hand. "I've never been ashamed of you," she told her. "Sad, afraid, worried about you...but never ashamed."

Rose nodded. "Storm called me last week and offered to pay the rent on an apartment for a year...with the condition that I take classes at the community college...and pass them. He said he didn't care what I studied, but that I had to learn some sort of trade. It feels like I'm accepting a handout I don't deserve, but if I'm ever going to get my life back on track, I have to take it."

Jane's eyes filled with tears as she stared at the man she loved more with every passing day. "I'm glad," she whispered. "I've only wanted you to be happy," she told Rose.

"I'm not there yet, but I'm working on it."

"Come on," Storm said from the kitchen. "Dinner's not going to cook itself. You can season the steaks."

Jane watched as her daughter sauntered over to where Storm was standing in the kitchen and knew she'd never forget this moment. Storm loved her enough to do whatever he could to help her daughter, even though she wasn't his favorite person.

* * * *

Later that night, Storm climbed into bed and took Jane into his arms.

She immediately turned and threw her leg over his hips to straddle him. They were both naked, as they'd found they loved sleeping skin to skin against each other. Even if they didn't make love, he loved feeling her against him that way.

He gripped her hips and looked up at her as she smiled at him.

"Thank you," she told him quietly.

Knowing what she was talking about, Storm simply said, "You're welcome."

"I can't believe you'd do that for Rose."

"I didn't do it for *her*," Storm told her, being honest. "I did it for *you*. She's your flesh and blood, and she's old enough to either take the help I offered her and thank her lucky stars for it, or ignore it and stay in the hole of a life she's dug for herself...and kiss any chance of a relationship with her mother goodbye. Thankfully, she was smart enough to take the help."

"You're amazing," Jane told him.

Storm shrugged. "I'm selfish," he retorted.

"How so?" she asked.

"The happier you are, the more relaxed you are. And the happier I am. Helping Rose means you're less stressed. I'd do anything for you, Jane. I hope you know that."

"I do," she reassured him. "Although I feel as if I'm not doing enough for *you*."

Storm couldn't help but snort and shake his head. "Baby, you do more for me just being here than you'll ever know. I was only half living before you came along. Going through the motions of life. Everything seems brighter, more exciting now that you're at my side. I wasn't kidding when I told the vice admiral that I wasn't going to be in the Navy forever. Not too long ago, I couldn't think about retiring without having a panic attack. Now I can't wait to spend every minute of every day with you. Laughing and simply enjoying life."

Jane's eyes filled with tears, but she smiled at the same time. "I love you."

"And I love you," he returned immediately. His hands moved from her waist up her body until he was cupping her breasts. He gently tweaked her nipples, which made her sit up straighter and slightly arch her back.

"I'm thinking I need to give you a hell of a thank-you present," she said breathlessly.

"Nope," Storm told her, shaking his head. "You don't owe me a damn thing." He moved suddenly, dumping her onto her back on the mattress and rolling until she was under him. "How about I give *you* another present instead?"

"Storm," she protested as he inched his way down her body, heading for the folds between her legs.

"Yeah?" he asked distractedly as he inhaled deeply and nuzzled her inner thigh.

"Never mind," Jane said as he licked her soaking-wet sex.

"That's what I thought," he mumbled before he got to work showing the love of his life how happy he was to have her in his bed and in his heart.

* * * *

An hour later, and after Jane had been thoroughly ravished, and after she'd ridden her man until he'd exploded deep within her, she lay on his chest, sweaty and more than satisfied. She'd visited her gynecologist, and after discussing her options, she had decided to go with a contraceptive implant. Storm told her that he'd schedule a vasectomy soon so she didn't have to put extra hormones in her body. It was a generous and loving thing for him to do, and it made Jane adore him all the more.

She loved feeling Storm come inside her, loved how intimate the act was without a condom between them.

As she lay there in his arms, she couldn't help but think about how much her life had changed for the better.

"You *are* going to marry me at some point, aren't you?" Storm asked quietly.

Jane chuckled. "If you ask me properly, yeah," she told him.

"Oh, I'm gonna ask you properly," he retorted. "But it'll be when you least expect it, and it'll definitely be a proposal to remember."

"I don't need pomp and circumstance," she said. "I just need you."

"You've got me," he reassured her. "I feel like the luckiest guy in the world," he said after a minute.

"I think that's my line," Jane told him.

"Nope. You're so amazing, someone would've snatched you up before I had a chance," he said, and Jane could tell he believed that with all his heart. "I'll spend the rest of my days making sure you don't regret loving me. I'll never hurt you. Never disrespect you. And I'll do whatever it takes to make sure you're safe and loved every day of your life."

His words were better than any marriage vows he could've recited to her.

Jane turned her head and kissed the underside of his jaw before snuggling back up against him. "That's all I could ask," she said. "All any woman could ask. I love you."

"Love you back."

"Get busy livin', or get busy dyin'," she said softly. "Just like Red did at the end of *Shawshank.*"

"Yup. Sleep now, baby. We have a long day tomorrow. Wolf and his team got jealous that they didn't get to spend a night eating with you, so they insisted we go over to his place for a day-long barbeque. And he's invited everyone on his team. Wives, children…hell, I think some of their pets will even be there."

Jane smiled. "You didn't tell me about this."

"I just did," Storm retorted. "They all love you. You're a part of our team now. You need them, they're there, just as Bubba, Rocco, and Gumby were not too long ago. If you can't get ahold of me, you call one of them. Any of them will do what they can to get to you. Understand?"

Jane nodded.

There were a ton of things she had to do. To talk to Storm about. Moving out of her apartment, Rose, their future, but at the moment, she was too tired, happy, and sated to do more than sigh against him and tighten her hold.

"Good night, baby," he said quietly.

"Good night, Storm."

Jane managed to stay awake long enough to hear Storm gently snoring under her cheek. She never would've thought this was where she'd eventually be when she'd stared at the handsome admiral every time she saw him in the hallways. But now that he was hers, she'd fight to keep him.

She turned her head, kissed his shoulder, then closed her eyes, content in the knowledge that she was loved.

* * * *

Also from 1001 Dark Nights and Susan Stoker, discover Rescuing Macie and Rescuing Sadie.

Keep reading for an exclusive excerpt from Finding Elodie, the first book in the new SEAL Team Hawaii Series!

Sign up for the 1001 Dark Nights Newsletter
and be entered to win a Tiffany Key necklace.

There's a contest every month!

Go to www.1001DarkNights.com to subscribe.

**As a bonus, all subscribers can download
FIVE FREE exclusive books!**

Discover 1001 Dark Nights Collection Eight

DRAGON REVEALED by Donna Grant
A Dragon Kings Novella

CAPTURED IN INK by Carrie Ann Ryan
A Montgomery Ink: Boulder Novella

SECURING JANE by Susan Stoker
A SEAL of Protection: Legacy Series Novella

WILD WIND by Kristen Ashley
A Chaos Novella

DARE TO TEASE by Carly Phillips
A Dare Nation Novella

VAMPIRE by Rebecca Zanetti
A Dark Protectors/Rebels Novella

MAFIA KING by Rachel Van Dyken
A Mafia Royals Novella

THE GRAVEDIGGER'S SON by Darynda Jones
A Charley Davidson Novella

FINALE by Skye Warren
A North Security Novella

MEMORIES OF YOU by J. Kenner
A Stark Securities Novella

SLAYED BY DARKNESS by Alexandra Ivy
A Guardians of Eternity Novella

TREASURED by Lexi Blake
A Masters and Mercenaries Novella

THE DAREDEVIL by Dylan Allen
A Rivers Wilde Novella

BOND OF DESTINY by Larissa Ione
A Demonica Novella

THE CLOSE-UP by Kennedy Ryan
A Hollywood Renaissance Novella

MORE THAN POSSESS YOU by Shayla Black
A More Than Words Novella

HAUNTED HOUSE by Heather Graham
A Krewe of Hunters Novella

MAN FOR ME by Laurelin Paige
A Man In Charge Novella

THE RHYTHM METHOD by Kylie Scott
A Stage Dive Novella

JONAH BENNETT by Tijan
A Bennett Mafia Novella

CHANGE WITH ME by Kristen Proby
A With Me In Seattle Novella

THE DARKEST DESTINY by Gena Showalter
A Lords of the Underworld Novella

Also from Blue Box Press

THE LAST TIARA by M.J. Rose

THE CROWN OF GILDED BONES by Jennifer L. Armentrout
A Blood and Ash Novel

THE MISSING SISTER by Lucinda Riley

Discover More Susan Stoker

Rescuing Macie
A Delta Force Heroes Novella

After years of estrangement, Mercedes Laughlin has finally reconcile with her older brother. It should be the happiest time of her life, gettin to know Truck and his new wife...and it would be, if an ex wasn't causin her trouble. Add in Truck's boss, Colonel Colton Robinson, an amazingl distracting man whom she met under embarrassing circumstances, an Macie's got a bit more on her plate than she can handle.

From the moment they met, Colt was fascinated by Macie, an helping her through an anxiety attack at her brother's wedding didn' diminish the appeal. He'd do his best to sweep her off her feet, if not fo a little voice telling him to tread lightly—until a frantic phone call change the plan. Macie's being targeted, and Colt's determined to keep her saf while he and her brother eliminate the threat.

Colt isn't about to let his friend lose his sister again so soon...or mis his own chance at a happy ending with Macie before they've barely had beginning.

* * * *

Rescuing Sadie
A Delta Force Heroes/Masters and Mercenaries Novella

Sadie Jennings was used to being protected. As the niece of Sear Taggart and the receptionist at McKay-Taggart Group, she was constantl surrounded by Alpha men more than capable, and willing, to lay dowr their lives for her. But when she visits her friend in San Antonio and act on suspicious activity at Milena's workplace, Sadie puts both of them ir the crosshairs of a madman. After several harrowing weeks, her friend i now safe, but for Sadie, the repercussions of her rash act linger on.

Chase Jackson, no stranger to dangerous situations as a captain in the

JS Army, has volunteered himself as Sadie's bodyguard. He fell head over
eels for the beautiful woman the first time he laid eyes on her. With a
)elta Force team at his back, he reassures the Taggarts that Sadie will be
afe. But when the situation in San Antonio catches up with her, Chase
as to use everything he's learned over his career to keep his promise...and
o keep Sadie alive long enough to officially make her his.

Finding Elodie
SEAL Team Hawaii
By Susan Stoker
Coming April 13, 2021

Read on for an excerpt from *Finding Elodie*, the first book in Stoker's SEAL Team Hawaii Series. You were briefly introduced to the Hawaiian team in this book…Mustang, Midas, Aleck, Pid, Jag, and Slate. This is Mustang's story.

Elodie, who is going by the name Rachel, is the cook on a cargo ship that has just been taken over by pirates. Mustang and his SEAL team are assigned to infiltrate the ship and eliminate the threat to the employees on board. This except starts at the moment Elodie first makes contact with the man who will end up changing her life.

* * * *

It was lucky the SEAL team was already in the area and could be taken off their previous mission. The team had been on a few cargo ships in the past and knew they were full of corridors and nooks and crannies. As much as Mustang hated that the crew members onboard the *Asaka Express* were probably scared out of their minds, he was looking forward to the challenge of finding, and taking out, each and every pirate.

"Sorry to interrupt, Sir," a lieutenant said as he stuck his head inside the door.

"What is it?" the admiral asked.

"We have communication from the *Asaka Express*."

"Thank fuck," Midas said.

"Can it be patched through?" the admiral asked.

"Yes, Sir. Just a moment." The lieutenant disappeared from the doorway once more.

Mustang and his team waited impatiently for the connection to be made to the cargo ship. When the sophisticated radio in the middle of the table finally squawked, Mustang blinked in surprise at the voice on the other end.

"Hello? Is anyone there?"

"Yes, ma'am, you've been connected. Please tell the admiral what you just told me."

"Um…okay. I'm on the *Asaka Express* and there are pirates onboard. We need help." The woman's voice was shaking, she was obviously scared, but she was keeping her composure.

"This is Admiral Light, I'm in charge of the *USS Paul Hamilton*. We're headed in your direction. What is your name?"

"El— Um…Rachel Walters."

Mustang looked over at Jag, who raised an eyebrow at hearing her response. Most people didn't stumble over their own name. Even in an extremely stressful situation like the one Ms. Walters had found herself in.

"And in what capacity do you work onboard?"

"My job? I'm the cook."

It wasn't unheard of to have females onboard the large cargo ships that constantly sailed through the waters in the Middle East, but it was still rare enough to be interesting.

"What can you tell us about the situation?" Admiral Light asked.

"Right, um, well, I can only tell you what I've heard. I—"

"What do you mean, you heard?" Mustang asked, interrupting her.

"Oh, uh…there're more than just the admiral there?" she asked.

"Yes," Mustang answered. "My SEAL team is here and we're going to come help you, but we need as much information as you can give us before we do. How many pirates are onboard?"

"Here's the thing," Rachel said. "I haven't actually *seen* any of them. They have pretty thick accents and it's hard for me to understand them. Walter…er…Captain Conger told everyone onboard to hide, so that's what I did. I'm in the galley…well, not the galley, but in one of the pantries nearby. I've got a radio, and one of the officers must've turned on a radio on the bridge, because it's been broadcasting. I can hear everything that's going on up there, but again, it's hard to understand. I can't see what's happening."

"How many crew are onboard?" Aleck asked.

"Twenty-two, including me," Rachel answered without hesitation.

"What channel were you listening to the bridge on?" Pid asked.

"Ten."

"And what channel are you on now?" Pid asked.

"Um…five, I think. I was just changing channels and seeing if anyone could hear me when you guys answered."

Pid reached into his pack on the floor and started rummaging around. He was the team's electronics expert, and Mustang knew he was going to try to tap into the radio frequency Rachel was using and listen to what was happening on the bridge of the *Asaka Express* himself.

"If you had to guess, how many men would you say boarded the ship?" the admiral asked.

Mustang heard Rachel sigh. "I don't know," she said. "We were all sleeping when it happened and woke when the captain made an announcement, telling us what was going on. But I think it's more than just a handful. There was talk of searching the ship earlier, and I'm not sure they'd do that if they only had three or four people, but I'm not an expert on forcefully taking over a ship, so I don't know for sure. They want money, and for the captain to open the containers. They said something about more men coming onboard when we got somewhere and that they didn't want hostages."

Not wanting hostages could be good or bad. It could mean the pirates really did just want money and valuables. After the *Maersk Alabama* incident, when the pirate in charge had been taken back to the States and thrown in prison and his comrades had been killed, hostage-taking by pirates had fallen out of favor. But not taking hostages could also mean the lives of every single one of the crew were in danger. It was easier to shoot to kill than to try to wrangle two dozen men.

And Mustang really didn't want to think about what they'd do to a woman if they found her onboard.

"Oh, crap...I hear something!" Rachel said.

"Stay quiet, turn down the volume on your radio, but don't disconnect," Mustang ordered.

"Okay...um...can I ask your name? I just...it feels more personal."

"I'm Mustang," he told her. "And my team is all here. Midas, Aleck, Pid, Jag, and Slate."

There was silence for a second, then a slight huff of breath. "I had to ask," she muttered.

Mustang hadn't thought twice about sharing his team's nicknames, but he'd forgotten how weird they'd sound to a civilian. "Scott," he said quietly. "My name is Scott."

"Scott. Okay," she whispered, then inhaled sharply as a loud bang sounded through the connection.

All six SEALs leaned forward, as if that could somehow help keep the woman on the other end of the line safe from whatever was happening. Admiral Light sat tense in his chair as he listened as well.

They could all hear raised voices in the background. Mustang closed his eyes and tried to distinguish what language was being spoken. He wasn't a language expert, but it sounded like a mix of Arabic and French to him.

"Stop pushing me!" a man's voice said in English.

Rachel's breathing was loud and fast. Mustang wanted to comfort her. Tell her to slow her breathing before she passed out, but he didn't dare say a word in case it would give away her hiding place.

"There's no one here," said the man speaking English.

"Men will regret not show themselves," a man said, obviously one of the pirates by the sound of his accent.

"Where more food?" another man asked.

"There are a few freezers in this hallway," the crew member said, "and more storage, but the best bet for stuff that can be eaten quickly, without having to cook it, is in the pantries on either side of the galley. That's where the snacks and things are kept. Back here is mostly flour, sugar, stuff like that. Things the cook uses to make the meals."

"Show us these pantries. And no try anything."

"I'm not," the officer said. "I'm doing exactly what you've told me."

"We come back for water and food," one of the pirates said. "We took more for money now."

Everyone in the conference room strained to listen for footsteps retreating, or for more conversation, but all they could hear were Rachel's terrified breaths.

"You're okay," Mustang said softly after a long moment, not able to keep quiet any longer. "They didn't find you."

"I know," she whispered back in a voice so low, everyone had to struggle to hear.

"Who was that?" Midas asked.

"I think it was Bryce…he's one of the officers who works with the captain on the bridge."

Mustang saw the admiral writing the name down, though he was sure someone was working on getting a list of every crew member onboard the *Asaka Express*.

"Had you heard either of those two pirates before?" Aleck asked.

"I don't know. I'm sorry. God, I wish I was better at this," she moaned.

"You're doing fine," Mustang reassured her.

"I'm not. So far I've told you nothing you probably didn't already know," she said.

"Other than the original distress call, you're the first communication we've had from your ship," Mustang countered.

"I am?" Rachel asked. "That's weird. I mean, we've all been trained to use the radios to call for help."

"Are the others in the engine room or in the bowels of the ship?" Pid asked.

"Probably both, but I'm guessing most are in the engine room. It's loud down there and easier to hide. A cough or movement can more easily be masked by the noise of the engines," Rachel said.

"And being lower in the ship, surrounded by all the steel, makes it more difficult for radio transmissions to get through on a handheld radio," Pid told her.

"I guess that makes sense," Rachel mused.

"Why aren't *you* in the engine room?" Mustang couldn't help but ask.

"I'm the cook," Rachel told him, as if that explained everything.

"And?" Slate asked.

"And depending on how long the pirates are here, the guys are gonna need food and water."

Mustang shook his head. He was impressed with Rachel's dedication to her job, but she was putting herself in danger. Someone should've realized that, besides the captain, Rachel was probably the most vulnerable on that ship. The pirates could use her to force the other crew members to do their bidding.

He didn't even want to think of all the other ways they could use and abuse her.

* * * *

Getting Elodie off the ship safely is just the beginning of the story. Find out how their relationship progresses in Finding Elodie.

About Susan Stoker

New York Times, USA Today, #1 Amazon Bestseller, and *Wall Street Journal* Bestselling Author, Susan Stoker has a heart as big as the state of Tennessee where she lives, but this all American girl has also spent the last eighteen years living in Missouri, California, Colorado, Indiana, and Texas. She's married to a retired Army man (and current firefighter/EMT) who now gets to follow her around the country.

She debuted her first series in 2014 and quickly followed that up with the SEAL of Protection Series, which solidified her love of writing and creating stories readers can get lost in.

Connect with her at www.StokerAces.com

Discover More 1001 Dark Nights

BRIDE by Carly Phillips ~ INDULGE ME by J. Kenner ~ THE KING by Jennifer L. Armentrout ~ QUIET MAN by Kristen Ashley ~ ABANDON by Rachel Van Dyken ~ THE OPEN DOOR by Laurelin Paige~ CLOSER by Kylie Scott ~ SOMETHING JUST LIKE THIS by Jennifer Probst ~ BLOOD NIGHT by Heather Graham ~ TWIST OF FATE by Jill Shalvis ~ MORE THAN PLEASURE YOU by Shayla Black ~ WONDER WITH ME by Kristen Proby ~ THE DARKEST ASSASSIN by Gena Showalter

COLLECTION SEVEN
THE BISHOP by Skye Warren ~ TAKEN WITH YOU by Carrie Ann Ryan ~ DRAGON LOST by Donna Grant ~ SEXY LOVE by Carly Phillips ~ PROVOKE by Rachel Van Dyken ~ RAFE by Sawyer Bennett ~ THE NAUGHTY PRINCESS by Claire Contreras ~ THE GRAVEYARD SHIFT by Darynda Jones ~ CHARMED by Lexi Blake ~ SACRIFICE OF DARKNESS by Alexandra Ivy ~ THE QUEEN by Jen Armentrout ~ BEGIN AGAIN by Jennifer Probst ~ VIXEN by Rebecca Zanetti ~ SLASH by Laurelin Paige ~ THE DEAD HEAT OF SUMMER by Heather Graham ~ WILD FIRE by Kristen Ashley ~ MORE THAN PROTECT YOU by Shayla Black ~ LOVE SONG by Kylie Scott ~ CHERISH ME by J. Kenner ~ SHINE WITH ME by Kristen Proby

DISCOVER BLUE BOX PRESS
TAME ME by J. Kenner ~ TEMPT ME by J. Kenner ~ DAMIEN by J. Kenner ~ TEASE ME by J. Kenner ~ REAPER by Larissa Ione ~ THE SURRENDER GATE by Christopher Rice ~ SERVICING THE TARGET by Cherise Sinclair ~ THE LAKE OF LEARNING by Steve Berry and MJ Rose ~ THE MUSEUM OF MYSTERIES by Steve Berry and MJ Rose ~ TEASE ME by J. Kenner ~ FROM BLOOD AND ASH by Jennifer L. Armentrout ~ QUEEN MOVE by Kennedy Ryan ~ THE HOUSE OF LONG AGO by Steve Berry and MJ Rose ~ THE BUTTERFLY ROOM by Lucinda Riley ~ A KINGDOM OF FLESH AND FIRE by Jennifer L. Armentrout

On Behalf of 1001 Dark Nights,

Liz Berry, M.J. Rose, and Jillian Stein would like to thank ~

Steve Berry
Doug Scofield
Benjamin Stein
Kim Guidroz
Social Butterfly PR
Ashley Wells
Asha Hossain
Chris Graham
Chelle Olson
Kasi Alexander
Jessica Johns
Dylan Stockton
Richard Blake
and Simon Lipskar

Made in the USA
Columbia, SC
28 February 2022